SNAP SHOTS—

The man stood at the window, peering across the street at the photographer's shop. He lighted a cigar and then crossed the room to where the rifle was standing against the wall. He picked up the gun and studied it, then he carried it to the window and rested it on the sill. He focused the sight on the door of the shop, so that the crosshairs were on the center of the doorway. Then he sat back to wait.

The front door of the shop opened, and, one by one, the wedding party began pouring through the door.

Where the hell was Tommy Giordano? Was that . . . ? No. Not him. The sniper held his breath. At last Tommy appeared in the doorway.

One, Two . . . now!
He squeezed the trigger, pulling off two shots in rapid succession, sending cold lead flying straight for Tommy's head. . . .

More SIGNET Fiction

'Til Death

An 87th Precinct Mystery

by ED McBAIN

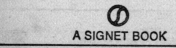

A SIGNET BOOK

NEW AMERICAN LIBRARY

SIGNET TRADEMARK REG. U.S. PAT. OFF. AND FOREIGN COUNTRIES
REGISTERED TRADEMARK—MARCA REGISTRADA
HECHO EN CHICAGO, U.S.A.

SIGNET, SIGNET CLASSIC, MENTOR, PLUME, MERIDIAN AND NAL
BOOKS are published by New American Library,
1633 Broadway, New York, New York 10019

FIRST PRINTING, FEBRUARY, 1975

5   6   7   8   9   10   11   12   13

PRINTED IN THE UNITED STATES OF AMERICA

This is for
MARGIE AND FRED

The city in these pages is imaginary.
The people, the places are all fictitious.
Only the police routine is based on established
investigatory technique.

► CAST OF CHARACTERS

CAST OF CHARACTERS

Chapter 1

DETECTIVE STEVE CARELLA blinked at the early Sunday morning sunshine, cursed himself for not having closed the blinds the night before, and then rolled over onto his left side. Relentlessly, the sunlight followed him, throwing alternating bars of black and gold across the white sheet. Like the detention cells at the 87th, he thought. God, my bed has become a prison.

No, that isn't fair, he thought. And besides, it'll all be over soon—but Teddy, I wish to hell you'd hurry.

He propped himself on one elbow and looked at his sleeping wife. Teddy, he thought. Theodora. Whom I used to call my *little* Theodora. How you have changed, my love. He studied her face, framed with short black hair recklessly cushioned against the stark white pillow. Her eyes were closed, thick-fringed with long black lashes. There was a faint smile on the full pout of her lips. Her throat swept in an immaculate arc to breasts covered by the sheet—and then the mountain began.

Really, darling, he thought, you do look like a mountain.

It is amazing how much you resemble a mountain. A very beautiful mountain, to be sure, but a mountain nonetheless. I wish I were a mountain climber. I wish, honey, oh how I wish I could get *near* you! How long has it been now? Cut it out, Steve-o, he told himself. Just cut it out because this sort of erotic rambling doesn't do anyone a damn bit of good, least of all me.

1

Steve Carella, the celebrated celibate.

Well, he thought, the baby is due at the end of the month, by God, that's next week! is it the end of June already? sure it is, my how the time flies when you've got nothing to do in bed but sleep. I wonder if it'll be a boy. Well, a girl would be nice, too, but oh would Papa raise a stink, he'd probably consider it a blot on Italy's honor if his only son Steve had a girl child first time out.

What were those names we discussed?

Mark if it's a boy and April if it's a girl. And Papa will raise a stink about the names, too, because he's probably got something like Rudolpho or Serafina in mind. Stefano Luigi Carella, that's me, and thank you, Pop.

Today is the wedding, he thought suddenly, and that makes me the most inconsiderate big brother in the world because all I can think of is my own libido when my kid sister is about to take the plunge. Well, if I know Angela, the prime concern on her mind today is probably *her* libido, so we're even.

The telephone rang.

It startled him for a moment, and he turned sharply toward Teddy, forgetting, thinking the sudden ringing would awaken her, and then remembering that his wife was a deaf mute, immune to little civilized annoyances like the telephone.

"I'm coming," he said to the persistent clamor. He swung his long legs over the side of the bed. He was a tall man with wide shoulders and narrow hips, his pajama trousers taut over a flat hard abdomen. Bare-chested and barefoot, he walked to the phone in nonchalant athletic ease, lifted the receiver, and hoped the call was not from the precinct. His mother would have a fit if he missed the wedding.

"Hello?" he said.

"Steve?"

"Yes. Who's this?"

"Tommy. Did I wake you?"

"No, no, I was awake." He paused. "How's the imminent bridegroom this morning?"

"I . . . Steve, I'm worried about something."

"Uh-oh," Carella said. "You're not planning on leaving my sister waiting at the altar, are you?"

"No, nothing like that. Steve, could you come over here?"

"Before we go to the church, you mean?"

"No. No, I mean now."

"Now?" Carella paused. A frown crossed his face. In his years with the police department, he had heard many anxious voices on the telephone. He had attributed the tone of Tommy's voice to the normal pre-conjugal jitters at first, but he sensed now that this was something more. "What is this?" he asked. "What's the matter?"

"I . . . I don't want to talk about it on the phone. Can you come over?"

"I'll be right there," he said. "As soon as I dress."

"Thank you, Steve," Tommy said, and he hung up.

Carella cradled the phone. He stared at it thoughtfully for a moment and then went into the bathroom to wash. When he came back into the bedroom, he tilted the blinds shut so that the sunshine would not disturb his sleeping wife. He dressed and wrote a note for her and then—just before he left—he caressed her breast with longing tenderness, sighed, and propped the note up against his pillow. She was still sleeping when he went out of the apartment.

Tommy Giordano lived alone in a private house in the suburb of Riverhead, not three miles from Carella's home. He was a Korean war veteran who'd had a macabre switch pulled on him while he was overseas. At a time when every American parent with a soldier son was worrying about mud and bullets, and every soldier son was worrying about Mongolian cavalry charges accompanied by the pounding of drums and the bleating of bugles—at a time like that, it was unthinkable to suppose that everyday living in the United States held its own nightmarish dangers. Tommy came to the realization with shocking suddenness.

His captain called him into the muddy command tent on a bleak rainy day. As gently as he knew how, he informed Tommy that both his parents had been killed in an automobile accident the day before, and that he was being flown home for the funeral. Tommy was an only child. He went home to watch them lower two people he had loved into the receptive earth, and then the Army flew him back to Korea again. He was despondent and uncommunicative throughout the remainder of the war. When he was finally discharged, he went back to the house he'd inherited from his parents. His only friend was a boy he'd known for years—until he met Angela Carella.

And one night, in Angela's arms, he cried bitterly, releasing the tears to which he could not succumb while wearing the uniform of a soldier. And then he was all right. And now he was Tommy Giordano, a pleasant-faced kid of twenty-seven with a disarming grin and an easygoing manner.

He opened the door the moment Carella rang as if he'd been waiting behind it, listening for the bell.

"Gee, Steve," he said, "I'm glad you came. Come on in. You want a drink or something?"

"At nine o'clock in the morning?" Carella asked.

"Is it that early? Gee, I must have got you out of bed. I'm sorry, Steve. I didn't mean to trouble you. A hell of a brother-in-law I'm going to make."

"Why'd you call, Tommy?"

"Sit down, Steve. You want some coffee? Have you had breakfast?"

"I can use a cup of coffee."

"Good. I'll make some toast, too. Look, I'm sorry as hell I woke you. I've been tossing and turning all night long myself. I guess I didn't realize how early it was. Man, this getting married is murder. I swear to God, I'd rather face a mortar attack."

"But this isn't why you called me."

"No. No, it's something else. I'm a little worried, to tell the truth, Steve. Not for myself, but for Angela. I mean, I just can't make it out."

"Make *what* out?"

"Well, like I said . . . listen, can you come in the kitchen? So I can make the coffee and toast? Would that be okay with you?"

"Sure."

They went into the kitchen. Carella sat at the table and lighted a cigarette. Tommy began measuring coffee into the percolator.

"I couldn't sleep all night," Tommy said. "I kept thinking of the honeymoon. When we're alone. What the hell do I do, Steve? I mean, I know she's your sister and all, but what do I do? How do I start? I love that girl. I don't want to hurt her or anything!"

"You won't. Just relax, Tommy. Just remember that you love her, and that you married her, and that you're going to be together for the rest of your lives."

"Gee, I'll tell you the truth, Steve, even *that* scares me."

"Don't let it." He paused. "Adam and Eve didn't have an instruction booklet, Tommy. And they made out all right."

"Yeah, well I hope so. I sure hope so. I just wish I knew what the hell to *say* to her." A pained look crossed his face, and Carella was momentarily amused.

"Maybe you won't have to say anything," Carella said. "Maybe she'll get the idea."

"Boy, I hope so." Tommy put the coffeepot on the stove and then slid two slices of bread into the toaster. "But I didn't call you so you could hold my hand. There's something else."

"What is it?"

"Well, I told you I couldn't sleep all night. So I guess I got up kind of early, and I went to take in the milk. They leave it right outside the door. When I first got out of the Army, I used to go down to the grocery store each morning. But now I have it delivered. It's a little more expensive, but . . ."

"Go ahead, Tommy."

"Yeah, well I was taking in the milk when I saw this little box resting on the floor, just outside the door."

"What kind of a box?"

"A little tiny box. Like the boxes rings come in, you know? So I picked it up and looked at it and there was a note on it."

"What did the note say?" Carella asked.

"Well, I'll show it to you in a few minutes. I took in the milk, and I carried the box into the bedroom. It was very nicely wrapped, Steve, fancy paper and a big bow and the note sticking up out of the bow. I couldn't figure out who'd left it. I thought it was probably a gag. One of the fellows. You know."

"Did you open it?"

"Yes."

"What was in it?"

"I'll let you see for yourself, Steve."

He walked out of the kitchen and through the apartment. Carella heard a drawer opening and then closing in the bedroom. Tommy came back into the kitchen. "Here's the note," he said.

Carella studied the handwritten message on the small rectangle:

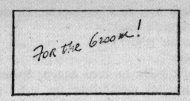

For the Groom!

"And the box?" he said.

"Here," Tommy said. He extended the small box to Carella. Carella put it on the kitchen table and lifted the lid. Then, quickly, he snapped the lid into place again.

Crouched in one corner of the box was a black widow spider.

Chapter 2

CARELLA SHOVED THE BOX away from him instantly. A look of utter horror had crossed his face, and it lingered still in his eyes and around the corners of his mouth.

"Yeah," Tommy said. "That's just the way I felt."

"You could have told me what was in the box," Carella said, beginning to think his future brother-in-law was something of a sadist. He had never liked spiders. During the war, stationed on a Pacific island, he had fought as bitterly against crawling jungle arachnids as he had against the Japanese. "You think this is a gag somebody played?" he asked incredulously.

"I did before I opened the box. Now I don't know. You'd have to have a pretty queer sense of humor to give somebody a black widow spider. Or *any* kind of a spider, for Christ's sake!"

"Is that coffee ready?"

"Just about."

"I'm really going to need a cup. Spiders have two effects on me. My mouth dries up, and I get itchy all over."

"I just get itchy," Tommy said. "When I was in basic training in Texas, we had to shake our shoes out every morning before we put them on. To make sure no tarantulas had crawled into them during the—"

"Please!" Carella said.

"Yeah, it gives you the creeps, don't it?"

"Do any of your friends have . . . odd senses of humor?" He swallowed hard. There seemed to be no saliva in his mouth.

"Well, I know some crazy people," Tommy said, "but this is a little far out, don't you think? I mean, this is slightly offbeat."

"Slightly," Carella said. "How's the coffee?"

"In a minute."

"Of course it *may* be a gag, who knows?" Carella said. "A sort of a wedding joke. After all, the spider is a classic symbol."

"Of what?"

"Of the vagina," Carella said.

Tommy blushed. A bright crimson smear started at his throat and quickly worked its way onto his face. If Carella had not seen it with his own eyes, he wouldn't have believed it. He quickly changed the topic.

"Or maybe it's just a feeble pun on marriage in general. You know. The female black widow is supposed to devour her mate."

Again Tommy blushed, and Carella realized there was no safe ground with a prospective bridegroom. Besides, he felt itchy. And his throat was dry. And no future brother-in-law had the goddamn right to spring a spider on a man so early in the morning—especially on Sunday morning."

"And of course," Carella went on, "there are more ominous overtones—if we're looking for them."

"Yeah," Tommy said. He glanced at the stove. "Coffee's ready." He carried the pot to the table and began pouring. "A gag is a gag, but suppose I'd reached into that box and got bit? The black widow is poisonous."

"Suppose *I'd* reached into it?" Carella asked.

"I wouldn't have let you, don't worry. But there was no one here when I opened it. I could've got bit."

"I doubt if it would have killed you."

"No, but it could have made me pretty sick."

"Maybe somebody wants you to miss your own wedding," Carella said.

"I thought of that. I also thought of something else."

"What?"

"Why send a black widow? A *widow,* do you follow me? It's almost as if . . . well . . . maybe it's a hint that Angela's gonna be a bride and a widow on the same day."

"You're talking like a man with a lot of enemies, Tommy."

"No. But I thought it might be a hint."

"A warning, you mean."

"Yes. And I've been wracking my brain ever since I opened that box, trying to think of anybody who'd . . . who'd want me dead."

"And who'd you come up with?"

"Only one guy. And he's three thousand miles away from here."

"Who?"

"A guy I knew in the Army. He said I was responsible for his buddy getting shot. I wasn't, Steve. We were on patrol together when a sniper opened up. I ducked the minute I heard the shot, and this other guy got hit. So his buddy claimed I was responsible. Said I should have yelled there was a sniper. How the hell was I supposed to yell it? I didn't even know it until I heard the shot—and then it was too late."

"Was the man killed?"

Tommy hesitated. "Yeah," he said at last.

"And his buddy threatened you?"

"He said he was gonna kill me one day."

"What happened after that?"

"He got shipped back home. Frostbite or something. I don't know. He lives in California."

"Have you ever heard from him since?"

"No."

"Was he the kind of a person who'd do a thing like this? Send a spider?"

"I didn't know him very well. From what I did know, he seemed like the kind of guy who *ate* spiders for breakfast."

Carella almost choked on his coffee. He put down his cup and said, "Tommy, I'm going to give you some advice. Angela is a very sensitive girl. I guess it runs in the Carella family. Unless you want to wind up getting a divorce real soon, I wouldn't discuss hairy or crawly or . . ."

"I'm sorry, Steve," Tommy said.

"Okay. What was this guy's name? The one who threatened you?"

"Sokolin. Marty Sokolin."

"Have any pictures of him?"

"No. What would I be doing with his picture?"

"Were you in the same company?"

"Yes."

"Do you have one of these company group pictures where everybody's grinning and wishing he was out of the Army?"

"No."

"Can you describe him?"

"He was a very big, beefy guy with a broken nose.

He looked like a wrestler. Black hair, very dark eyes. A small scar near his right eye. He was always smoking cigars."

"Think he had a police record?"

"I don't know."

"Well, we'll check on it." Carella was pensive for a moment. "It doesn't seem like, though, that he's the guy. I mean, what the hell, how would he know you were getting married today?" He shrugged. "Hell, this may just be a gag, anyway. Somebody with a warped sense of humor."

"Maybe," Tommy said, but he didn't seem convinced.

"Where's your phone?" Carella asked.

"In the bedroom."

Carella started out of the kitchen. He paused. "Tommy, would you mind a few extra guests at your wedding?" he asked.

"No. Why?"

"Well, if this *isn't* a gag—and it probably is—but if it isn't, we don't want anything happening to the groom, do we?" He grinned. "And the nice thing about having a cop for a brother-in-law is that he can get body-guards whenever he needs them. Even on a Sunday."

There is no such day as Sunday in the police department. Sunday is exactly the same as Monday and Tuesday and all those other days. If you happen to have the duty on Sunday, that's it. You don't go to the commissioner or the chaplain or the mayor. You go to the squadroom. If Christmas happens to fall on one of your duty days, that's extremely unfortunate, too, unless you can arrange a switch with a cop who isn't celebrating Christmas. Life is just one merry round in the police department.

On Sunday morning, June 22, Detective 2nd/Grade Meyer Meyer was catching in the squadroom of the 87th

Precinct. It was not a bad day to be in charge of the six-man detective team which had begun its shift at 8:00 A.M. and which would work through until 6:00 P.M. that evening. There was a mild breeze on the air, and the sky was a cloudless blue, and sunlight was pouring through the meshed grill screening over the squadroom's windows. The squadroom, shoddy with time and use, was quite comfortable on a day such as this. There were days when the city's temperature soared into the nineties, and on those days the squadroom of the 87th Precinct resembled nothing so much as a big iron coffin. But not today. Today, a man could sit without his trousers crawling up his behind. Today, a man could type up reports or answer phones or dig in the files without danger of melting into a small unidentifiable puddle on the squadroom floor.

Meyer Meyer was quite content. Puffing on his pipe, he studied the *Wanted* circulars on his desk and thought about how nice it was to be alive in June.

Bob O'Brien, six feet and one inch tall in his bare feet, weighing in at two hundred and ten pounds, stomped across the room and collapsed into the chair beside Meyer's desk. Meyer felt an immediate sense of doom, because if ever there was a jinxed cop it was O'Brien. Since the time he'd been forced to kill a neighborhood butcher years ago—a man he'd known since he was a boy —O'Brien seemed to find himself constantly in the kind of scrapes wherein gunplay was absolutely necessary. He had not wanted to kill Eddie the butcher. But Eddie'd been a little out of his head and had come raving out of his shop swinging a meat cleaver at an innocent woman. O'Brien tried to stop him, but it was no use. Eddie knocked him to the pavement and then raised the meat cleaver and O'Brien, acting reflexively, drew his service revolver and fired. He killed Eddie with a single shot. And that night he went home and wept like a baby. He had killed six men since that time. In each of the shootings, he had not wanted to draw his gun—but circumstances so combined to force him into the act of legal murder. And whenever he was forced to kill, he still wept. Not openly. He wept inside, where it hurts most.

The cops of the 87th Squad were not a superstitious bunch, but they nonetheless shied away from answering a complaint with Bob O'Brien along. With O'Brien along, there was bound to be shooting. They did not know why. It certainly wasn't Bob's fault. He was always the last person on the scene to draw a gun, and he never did so until it became absolutely necessary. But with O'Brien along, there would undoubtedly be shooting and the cops of the 87th were normal-type human beings who did not long to become involved in gun duels. They knew that if O'Brien went out to break up a marble game being played by six-year-old tots, one of those tots would miraculously draw a submachine gun and begin blasting away. That was Bob O'Brien. A hard-luck cop.

And that, of course, was pure police exaggeration because O'Brien had been a cop for ten years, four of them with the 87th, and he'd only shot seven men in all that time. Still, that was a pretty good average.

"How's it going, Meyer?" he asked.

"Oh, very nicely," Meyer said. "Very nicely, thank you."

"I've been wondering."

"What about?"

"Miscolo."

Miscolo was the patrolman in charge of the Clerical Office just down the corridor. Meyer very rarely wondered about him. In fact, he very rarely even thought about him.

"What's the matter with Miscolo?" he asked now.

"His coffee," O'Brien said.

"Something wrong with his coffee?"

"He used to make a good cup of coffee," O'Brien said

wistfully. "I can remember times, especially during the winter, when I'd come in here off a plant or something and there was a cup of Miscolo's coffee waiting for me and I'm telling you, Meyer, it made a man feel like a prince, a regular prince. It had rich body, and aroma, and flavor."

"You're wasting your time with police work," Meyer said. "I'm serious, Bob. You should become a television announcer. You can sell coffee the way . . ."

"Come on, I'm trying to be serious."

"Excuse me. So what's wrong with his coffee now?"

"I don't know. It just isn't the same any more. You know when it changed?"

"When?"

"When he got shot. Remember when that nutty dame was up here with a bottle of TNT and she shot Miscolo? Remember that time?"

"I remember," Meyer said. He remembered very well. He still had scars as mementos of the pistol whipping he'd received from Virginia Dodge on that day last October. "Yes, I remember."

"Well, right after Miscolo got out of the hospital, the first day he was on the job again, the coffee began to stink. Now what do you suppose causes something like that, Meyer?"

"Gee, I don't know, Bob."

"Because, to me, it's a phenomenon, I mean it. A man gets shot, and suddenly he can't make good coffee any more. Now, to me, that's one of the eight wonders of the world."

"Why don't you ask Miscolo?"

"Now how can I do that, Meyer? He takes pride in the cup of coffee he makes. Can I ask him how come his coffee is suddenly no good? How can I do that, Meyer?"

"I guess you can't."

"And I can't go out to *buy* coffee or he'll be offended. What should I do, Meyer?"

"Gee, Bob, I don't know. It seems to me you've got a problem. Why don't you try some occupational therapy?"

"Huh?"

"Why don't you call up some of the witnesses to that holdup we had the other day and see if you can't get something more out of them?"

"You think I'm goofing, you mean?"

"Did I say that, Bob?"

"I'm not goofing, Meyer," O'Brien said. "I've just got a thirst for some coffee, and the thought of drinking Miscolo's is making me sick."

"Have a glass of water instead."

"At nine-thirty in the morning?" O'Brien looked shocked. "Do you think we can call the desk and ask Murchison to sneak in some coffee from outside?"

The telephone on Meyer's desk rang. He snatched it from the cradle and said, "Eighty-seventh Squad, Detective Meyer."

"Meyer, this is Steve."

"Hi, boy. Lonely for the place, huh? Can't resist calling in even on your day off."

"It's your twinkling blue eyes I miss," Carella said.

"Yeah, everybody's charmed by my eyes. I thought your sister was getting married today."

"She is."

"So what can I do for you? Need a few bucks for a wedding present?"

"No. Meyer, would you take a look at the new schedule and see who's on my team this week? I want to know who else is off today."

"You need a fourth for bridge? Hold on a second." He opened his top desk drawer and pulled out a clipboard to which a mimeographed sheet was attached. He studied the grid, his index finger running down the page:

	Sunday 6/21	Monday 6/22	Tuesday 6/23	Wednesday 6/24	Thursday 6/25
8:00 AM to 6:00 PM	Meyer ● O'Brien Willis	Fields ● Di Maeo Levine	Carella ● Hawes Kling	Brown Meredith ● Kapek	Meyer ● O'Brien Willis
6:00 PM to 8:00 AM	Brown ● Meredith Kapek	Meyer ● O'Brien Willis	Fields ● Di Maeo Levine	Carella ● Hawes Kling	Brown Meredith ● Kapek
Off duty	Carella Hawes Kling	Brown Meredith Kapek	Meyer O'Brien Willis	Fields Di Maeo Levine	Carella Hawes Kling
Patrol Day	Fields Di Maeo Levine	Carella Hawes Kling	Brown Meredith Kapek	Meyer O'Brien Willis	Fields Di Maeo Levine

SPECIAL ASSIGNMENT: Alexander, Parker, Kasoukian, Masterson
● Catcher

"Oh, I pity these poor bastards," Meyer said into the phone. "Having to work with a *schnook* like . . ."

"Come on, come on, who are they?" Carella asked.

"Kling and Hawes."

"Have you got their home numbers handy?"

"Is there anything else you'd like, sir? Shoes shined? Pants pressed? Loan of my wife for the weekend?"

"Now that isn't a bad idea," Carella said, grinning.

"Hold on. You got a pencil to take this down?"

"Sarah's number?"

"Leave Sarah out of this."

"You were the one who brought her up."

"Listen, horny, you want these numbers or not? We're trying to run a tight little squad here."

"Shoot," Carella said, and Meyer gave him the numbers. "Thank you. Now there are a few more things I'd like you to do for me. First, will you see what you can get on a guy named Marty Sokolin. You may draw a blank because he's a resident of California and we haven't got time to check with the FBI. But give our own IB a buzz and see if he's turned up here in the past few years. Most important, try to find out if he's here now."

"I thought this was your day off," Meyer said wearily.

"A conscientious cop never has a day off," Carella said conscientiously. "The last thing is this. Can you send a patrolman over to my house to pick up a note? I'd like the lab to look it over, and I'd like a report on it as soon as possible."

"You think we're running a private messenger service here?"

"Come on, Meyer, loosen the reins. I should be home in a half-hour or so. Try to get back to me on Sokolin before noon, will you?"

"I'll try," Meyer said. "What else do you do for diversion on your day off? Pistol practice?"

"Goodbye, Meyer," Carella said. "I've got to call Bert and Cotton."

Cotton Hawes was dead asleep when the telephone rang in his bachelor apartment. He heard it only vaguely and then as a distant tinkle. During World War II, he'd been the only man aboard his PT boat who'd earned the distinction of having slept through the bleatings of the alarm announcing General Quarters. He'd almost lost his Chief Torpedoman's rating because of the incident. But the captain of the vessel was a lieutenant, j.g., who'd been trained as a radar technician for the Navy's Communications Division and who didn't know torpedoes from toenails. He recognized, with some injury to his ego, that the man who really commanded the boat, the man who established rapport with the crew, the man who knew navigation and ballistics, was really Cotton Hawes and not himself. The j.g. (anachronistically called "The Old Man" by the crew, even though he was only twenty-five years old) had been a disc jockey in his home town, Schenectady, New York. He wanted only to return safely to—in order of their importance—his beloved records, his beloved MG convertible, and his beloved Annabelle Tyler whom he'd been dating since high school. He did not appreciate Naval chains of command or Naval reprimands or Naval operations. He knew he had a job to do and he knew he could not do it without Cotton Hawes's complete co-operation. Perhaps the Admiral would have been delighted were Hawes demoted to Torpedoman First Class. The j.g. didn't much give a damn about the Admiral.

"You'll have to watch that stuff," he said to Hawes. "We can't have you sleeping through another kamikaze attack."

"No, sir," Hawes said. "I'm sorry, sir. I'm a heavy sleeper."

"I'm assigning a seaman to wake you whenever General Quarters is sounded. That should take care of it."

"Yes, sir," Hawes said. "Thank you, sir."

"How the hell did you manage to snore through that ungodly din, Cotton? We almost had two direct hits on our bow!"

"Mike, I can't help it," Hawes said. "I'm a heavy sleeper."

"Well, somebody'll wake you from now on," the j.g. said. "Let's come through this damn thing alive, huh, Cotton?"

They came through the damn thing alive. Cotton Hawes never heard from the j.g. after they were separated at Lido Beach. He assumed he'd gone back to jockeying discs in Schenectady, New York. And whereas the seaman had temporarily foiled the further attempts of Japanese pilots to sink the boat, the victory over Morpheus was at best a shallow one. Cotton Hawes was still a heavy sleeper. He attributed this to the fact that he was a big man, six feet two inches tall and weighing a hundred and ninety pounds. Big men, he maintained, needed a lot of sleep.

The telephone continued to tinkle somewhere in the far distance. There was movement on the bed, the creaking of springs, the rustle of the sheet being thrown back. Hawes stirred slightly. The distant tinkle was somewhat louder now. And then, added to the tinkle, came a voice fuzzy with sleep.

"Hello?" the voice said. "Who? I'm sorry, Mr. Carella, he's asleep. Can you call back a little later? Me? I'm Christine Maxwell." The voice paused. "No, I don't think I ought to wake him right now. Can he call you when he . . ." Christine paused again. Cotton sat up in bed. She stood naked at the telephone, the black receiver to her ear, her blond hair pushed back to tumble over the black plastic in a riot of contrast. Delightedly, he watched her, her slender fingers curled about the telephone, the curving sweep of her arm, the long length of her body. Her brow was knotted in a frown now. Her blue eyes were puzzled.

"Well," she said, "why didn't you say you were from the squad to begin with? Just a moment, I'll see if . . ."

"I'm up," Hawes said from the bed.

"Just a second," Christine said to the telephone. "He's coming now." She cradled the mouthpiece. "It's a Steve Carella. He says he's from the 87th Squad."

"He is," Hawes said, walking to the phone.

"Does that mean you'll have to go in today?"

"I don't know."

"You promised you'd spend the day . . ."

"I haven't even talked to him yet, honey." Gently, Hawes took the phone from her hand. "Hello, Steve," he said. He yawned.

"Did I get you out of bed?"

"Yes."

"You busy today?"

"Yes."

"Feel like doing me a favor?"

"No."

"Thanks a million."

"I'm sorry, Steve, I've got a date. I'm supposed to go on a boatride up the Harb."

"Can't you break it? I need help."

"If I break the date, the lady'll break my head." Christine, listening to the conversation, nodded emphatically.

"Come on. Big strong guy like you. You can take the girl with you."

"Take her where?"

"To my sister's wedding."

"I don't like weddings," Hawes said. "They make me nervous."

"Somebody's threatened my future brother-in-law. Or at least it looks that way. I'd like a few people I can trust in the crowd. Just in case anything happens. What do you say?"

"Well . . ." Hawes started. Christine shook her head. "No, Steve. I'm sorry."

"Look, Cotton, when's the last time I asked you for a favor?"

"Well . . ." Hawes started, and again Christine shook her head. "I can't, Steve."

"There'll be free booze," Carella said.

"No."

"Take the girl with you."

"No."

"Cotton, I'm asking a favor."

"Just a second," Hawes said, and he covered the mouthpiece.

"No," Christine said immediately.

"You're invited," Hawes said. "To a wedding. What do you say?"

"I want to go on the boatride. I haven't been on a boatride since I was eighteen."

"We'll go next Sunday, okay?"

"You're not off next Sunday."

"Well, the first Sunday I *am* off, okay?"

"No."

"Christine?"

"No."

"Honey?"

"Oh, damnit."

"All right?"

"Damnit," Christine said again.

"Steve," Hawes said into the phone, "we'll come."

"Damnit," Christine said.

"Where do you want us to meet you?"

"Can you come over to my place at about noon?"

"Sure. What's the address?"

"837 Dartmouth. In Riverhead."

"We'll be there."

"Thanks a lot, Cotton."

"Send flowers to my funeral," Hawes said, and he hung up.

Christine stood fuming by the telephone, her arms crossed over her breasts. Hawes reached for her and she said, "Don't touch me, Mr. Hawes."

"Honey . . ."

"Don't *honey* me."

"Christine, honey, he's in a jam."

"You promised we would go on this boatride. I made the arrangements *three weeks* ago. Now . . ."

"This is something I couldn't avoid. Look, Carella happens to be a friend of mine. And he needs help."

"And what am I?"

"The girl I love," Hawes said. He took her into his arms.

"Sure," Christine answered coldly.

"You know I love you." He kissed the tip of her nose.

"Sure. You love me, all right. I'm just the merry widow, to you. I'm just the girl you . . ."

"You're a very lovely widow."

". . . picked up in a bookshop."

"It's a very lovely bookshop," Hawes said, and he kissed the top of her head. "You've got nice soft hair."

"I'm not quite as alone in the world as you may think," Christine said, her arms still folded across her breasts. "I could have got a hundred men to take me on this boatride."

"I know," he said, and he kissed her earlobe.

"You louse," she said. "It just happens that I love you."

"I know." He kissed her neck.

"Stop that."

"Why?"

"You know why."

"Why?"

"Stop it," she said, but her voice was gentler, and her arms were beginning to relax. "We have to go to your friend's house, don't we?"

"Not until noon."

Christine was silent. "I do love you," she said.

"And I love you."

"I'll bet you do. I'll just bet you . . ."

"Shhh, shhh," he said, and he sought her mouth, and she brought her arms up around his neck. He clung to her, his big hands twisting in the long blond hair. He kissed her again, and she buried her face in his shoulder, and he said, "Come. Come with me."

"Your friend. There isn't time . . ."

"There's time."

"We have to . . ."

"There's time."

"But won't we . . . ?"

"There's time," he said gently.

———————

Bert Kling was reading the Sunday comics when Carella's call came. He took a last wistful look at Dick Tracy's wrist radio and then went to answer the phone.

"Bert Kling," he said.

"Hi, Bert. This is Steve."

"Uh-oh," Kling said immediately.

"You busy?"

"I won't answer any leading questions. What happened? What do you want?"

"Don't be so brusque. Brusqueness is not flattering to youth."

"Do I have to go to the squad?"

"No."

"What then?"

"My sister's getting married this afternoon. The groom received what could amount to a threatening note."

"Yeah? Why doesn't he call the police?"

"He did. And now I'm calling you. Feel like going to a wedding?"

"When? What time?"

"Can you be here at twelve?"

"I've got to pick up Claire at nine tonight. There's a movie she wants to see."

"Okay."

"Where are you now?" Kling asked.

"Home. 837 Dartmouth. In Riverhead. Can you be here by noon?"

"Yeah. I'll see you."

"Bert?"

"What?"

"Bring your gun."

"Okay," Kling said, and he hung up. He walked back to the newspaper. He was a tall blond man of twenty-five years, and he looked younger in his undershorts because his legs were covered with a light blond fuzz. He curled up in the armchair, studying the wrist radio design again, and then he decided to call Claire. He went to the telephone and dialed her number.

"Claire," he said, "this is Bert."

"Hello, lover."

"I'm going to a wedding this afternoon."

"Not your own, I hope."

"No. Steve's sister. You want to come?"

"I can't. I told you that I've got to drive my father out to the cemetery."

"Oh yeah, that's right. Okay, I'll see you at nine then, okay?"

"Right. This movie's at a drive-in. Is that all right?"

"That's fine. We can neck if it gets dull."

"We can neck even if it doesn't get dull."

"What's the picture anyway?"

"It's an old one," Claire said, "but I think you'll enjoy it."

"What is it?"

"*Dragnet,*" she answered.

The packet from the Bureau of Criminal Identification arrived at the squadroom at 10:37 A.M.

Meyer Meyer was, in truth, surprised to see it. The chances of this Marty Whatever-His-Name-Was having a record were pretty slim to begin with. Add to that the possibility of his having a record in *this* city, and the chances were beyond the realm of plausibility. But record he had, and the record was in the voluminous files of the IB, and now a photostated copy of the file rested on Meyer's desk, and he leafed through it leisurely.

Marty Sokolin was not a big-time thief. He wasn't even, by any police standards, a small-time thief. He was a man who'd got into trouble once. His record happened to be in the IB's files because he'd got into trouble in this city while on vacation from California.

It was perhaps significant that Marty Sokolin had not been discharged from the Army because of frostbite as Tommy Giordano had supposed. True enough, he had been medically discharged. But he'd been released to a mental hospital in Pasadena, California, as a neurasthenic patient.

Meyer Meyer knew nothing of Tommy's frostbite supposition. He knew, however, that neurasthenia was the modern psychiatric term for what, during World War I, had been called plain and simple "shell shock." A psychiatrist probably would have defined it as nervous debility or exhaustion, as from overwork or prolonged mental strain. Meyer simply called it "shell shock" and noted that Sokolin had been released from the hospital as fit to enter society in the summer of 1956.

He did not have his brush with the law until almost two years later in March of 1958. He'd been working, at the time, as a salesman for a paint company in San Francisco. He'd come East for a sales convention and had begun drinking with a stranger in a midtown bar. At some point during the evening, the conversation had swung around to the Korean War. The stranger had admitted that he'd been 4-F and rather glad of it. Because of his disability, a slight heart murmur, he'd been able to make fantastic advances in his company while men of his own age were away fighting.

Sokolin had at first reacted to the man's confession with slightly drunken solemnity bordering on the maudlin. One of his best friends, he informed the stranger, had been killed in Korea because another soldier had failed to do his duty. The stranger sympathized, but his sympathy must have sounded hollow and insincere to Sokolin. Before the stranger fully realized what was happening, Sokolin was hurling curses at him for being a deserter and a shirker and another son of a bitch who didn't do his duty when he saw it. The stranger tried to get away, but Sokolin's ire mounted irrationally until finally he smashed a beer mug on the edge of the bar and came at the stranger with the broken shard clutched in his fist.

He did not kill the surprised 4-Fer, but he did manage to cut him badly. And perhaps the attack would have been considered second-degree assault had not Sokolin accompanied it with eight words spoken clearly and distinctly in the presence of the half-dozen witnesses lining the bar.

Those words were: "I'll kill you, you son of a bitch!"

And so the assault had leaped into the rarefied atmosphere bounded by the words "with an intent to kill a human being," and the indictment read first-degree, and the maximum penalty for violation of Section 240 of the Penal Law was ten years in prison as opposed to the maximum five years for the second-degree crime.

Sokolin had come off pretty well. He was a war veteran, and this was a first offense. It was, nonetheless, first-degree assault and the judge could not let him off with a fine and a fatherly pat on the head. He was found guilty and sentenced to two years in Castleview Prison upstate. He'd been an ideal prisoner. He'd applied for a parole after serving a year of his term, and the parole had been granted as soon as a firm job offer was presented to the board. He had been released from Castleview two months ago—on April 3.

Meyer Meyer pulled the phone to him and dialed Carella's home number. Carella answered the phone on the third ring.

"I've got that stuff you wanted on Sokolin," Meyer said. "Did that patrolman show up for the note yet?"

"About a half-hour ago," Carella said.

"Well, he's not back here yet. You're leaving about noon, huh?"

"About one o'clock, actually."

"Where can I reach you if the lab comes up with something?"

"The wedding's at three at the Church of the Sacred Heart at the intersection of Gage and Ash in Riverhead. The reception starts at five at my mother's house. It's gonna be an outdoor thing."

"What's the address there?"

"831 Charles Avenue."

"Okay. You want this stuff on Sokolin?"

"Give it to me."

Meyer gave it to him.

When he'd finished talking, Carella said, "So he's on parole now, huh? Went back to California with a firm job offer."

"No, Steve. I didn't say that."

"Then where is he?"

"Right here. The job offer came from this city."

Chapter 3

BY ONE-THIRTY that bright Sunday afternoon, Antonio
Carella was ready to shoot his wife, strangle his son, disown his daughter, and call off the whole damn wedding.

To begin with, Tony was paying for the wedding. This
was the first time—and the last time, thank God—a
daughter of his was getting married. When Steve married
Teddy, it was *her* parents who had paid for the festivities.
Not so this time. This time, Tony was shelling out, and
he was discovering that the wedding would cost, at a con-
servative estimate, just about half what he earned in an
entire year at his bakery.

The biggest of the thieves, and he had half a mind to
ask Steve to arrest the crooks, were the men who called
themselves Weddings–Fetes, Incorporated. They had arrived at the Charles Avenue address at 9:00 A.M. that
morning (after Tony had stayed up all night in the bakery
getting his Sunday morning breads baked) and proceeded
to turn the Carella backyard into a shambles. The Carella
house in Riverhead was a small one, but the land on
which it rested was possibly the largest plot on the street,
stretching back from the house in a long rectangle which
almost reached the next block. Tony was very proud of
his land. His back yard boasted a grape arbor which
rivaled any to be found in his home town of Marsala. He
had planted fig trees, too, nourished them with loving

care, pruned them in the summer, wrapped them with protective tarpaulin in the winter. And now these crooks, these *brigandi,* were trampling over his lawn with their tables and their ridiculous flags and flower canopies and . . .

"Louisa!" he had screamed to his wife. "Why inna hell we can't hire a hall? Why inna hell we have to have a *outdoor* wedding! A hall was good enough for me, an' good enough for you, an' good enough for my son, but Angela has to have a outdoor wedding! So those crooks can tear up my lawn an' ruin my grapes an' my figs! *Pazzo! E proprio pazzo!"*

"Shut up," Louisa Carella said kindly. "You'll wake up the whole house."

"The whole house is wake up already!" Tony said. "Besides, there's nobody in the whole house but me, you, an' Angela, an' she's getting married today an' she's not sleeping, anyway!"

"The caterers will hear you," Louisa said.

"For what I'm paying them, they're entitled to hear," Tony replied, and grumblingly he had got out of bed and gone down to the back yard to supervise the setting of the tables and the construction of the bridal arbors and bandstand and dance floor. The caterers, he discovered, were very fancy people. Not only were they turning his back yard into a Hollywood set for *Father of the Bride* (starring *me,* Antonio Carella, he thought sourly) but they were also building a twelve-foot mermaid, the length of the young fish-woman's body to be sculpted from ice, a similarly sculpted ice tub to rest beneath her and contain bottles of champagne for any thirsty guests. Tony prayed to God the sun would not get too strong. He visualized the fish-woman melting into the tub, the champagne beginning to taste like lukewarm ginger ale.

At one o'clock, his son and daughter-in-law arrived. Now Steve was a boy Tony could usually count on. Before Steve had gone into the Army, he used to work nights at the bakery, even though he was going to college during the day. Steve was a boy who could be trusted. He was a boy a father could count on. So today—*San Giacinto di California!*—even Steve had turned on him. Today, of all days, with those thieving Weddings–Fetes, Incorporated, tearing up the lawn, with Angela running around like a chicken *senza capo,* with the world of Antonio Carella slowly collapsing around him, his own true son Steve had arrived at the house with three additional guests! Not that Tony minded the extra expense. No, that didn't matter to him at all. So he would work an additional four months in the bakery to make up the money. But it was having to explain to these Incorporateds that there would be three more people and that they would have to arrange them at different tables. Steve was insistent on that. No, he did not want to sit with his friends. He wanted one here, and one here, and himself over there! *Pazzo!* His own son, as crazy as all the others.

And the tall one, the redheaded one with the white streak in his hair—*sangue della maruzza!* He was enough to frighten all the bridesmaids in Riverhead. And Tony was sure he had seen a gun under the redhead's coat when he stooped down to tie his shoe. A big black revolver sticking out of a shoulder holster. All right, it was a good thing for his son to be a cop, but did his friends have to carry weapons to a peaceful Christian wedding?

And then Angela had started. At one-fifteen, exactly one hour and forty-five minutes before the wedding, she had begun to cry as if the world was trying to rape her. Louisa had come running out back, wringing her hands.

"Stevie," she said, "go up to her. Tell her it'll be all right, will you? Go. Go to your sister."

Tony had watched his son go upstairs. That wailing from the upper-story bedroom window had not ceased. Tony sat with his daughter-in-law Teddy—*com'é grande,* he thought, *povera Theodora!*—and the three strangers, Mr. Hawes, Mr. Kling, and Miss Maxwell, drinking wine and ready to shoot his wife, strangle his son, disown his daughter, and call off the whole damn wedding!

He fumed and fretted until Teddy patted his hand. And then he smiled at her, and nodded his head, and rested his hands on his paunch and hoped—please, dear God!—that everything would turn out all right and that somehow he, Antonio Carella, would survive the day.

Standing in the corridor outside Angela's bedroom, Carella could hear his sister sobbing beyond the door. He knocked gently and then waited.

"Who is it?" Angela said, her voice breaking.

"Me. Steve."

"What do you want?"

"Come on, Slip, open up."

"Go away, Steve."

"You can't chase me away. I'm a police officer investigating a disturbance of the peace." He wasn't quite sure, but he thought he heard his sister stifle a laugh on the other side of the door. "Slip?" he said.

"What?"

"Do I have to kick it in?"

"Oh, wait a minute," Angela said. He heard footsteps approaching the door. The bolt was slipped, but Angela did not open the door for him. He heard her footsteps retreating and then the bedsprings creaking as she hurled herself down. He eased the door open and entered the room. Angela was lying full length on the bed, her face buried in the pillow. She wore a full white slip and her brown hair tumbled to her shoulders in a riot of disarray. Her slip had pulled back to reveal a blue garter taut around her nylon.

"Pull down your dress," Carella said. "Your behind is showing."

"It's not a dress," Angela said poutingly. "It's a slip. And who asked you to look?" but she pulled it down over her leg instantly.

Carella sat on the edge of the bed. "What's the trouble?"

"There's no trouble." She paused. "There's no trouble at all." And then she sat up suddenly, turning her brown eyes toward her brother, surprisingly Oriental eyes in a high cheek-boned face, the face a refinement of Carella's, pretty with an exotic tint that spoke of Arabian visits to the island of Sicily in the far distant past. "I don't want to marry him," she said. She paused. "That's the trouble."

"Why not?"

"I don't love him."

"Oh, bullshit," Carella said.

"I don't like swearing, Steve. You know that. I never could stand swearing, even when we were kids. You used to swear on purpose, just to annoy me. That, and calling me 'Slip.' "

"You started the 'slip' business," Carella said.

"I did not," Angela told him. "You did. Because you were mean and rotten."

"I was telling you the truth," Carella said.

"It's not nice to tell a thirteen-year-old girl that she's not really a girl because she still wears cotton slips."

"I was helping you on the road to maturity. You asked Mama to buy you some nylon slips after that, didn't you?"

"Yes, and she refused."

"It was in the right direction."

"You gave me an inferiority complex."

"I gave you an insight into the mysterious ways of womanhood."

"Oh, bullshit," Angela said, and Carella laughed aloud. "It's not funny. I'm not going to marry him. I don't like anything about him. He's a worse boor than you are. And he swears more. And besides . . ." She stopped. "Stevie, I'm afraid. Stevie, I don't know what to do. I'm terrified."

"Come on," he said, "come on," and he took his sister

into his arms and stroked her hair and said, "There's nothing to be afraid of."

"Steve, he's *killed* people, do you know that?"

"So have I."

"I know, but . . . we're going to be alone tonight in . . . in one of the biggest hotels in the world . . . right in this city . . . and I don't even know the man I'm about to marry. How can I allow him to . . . to . . ."

"Did you talk to Mama, Slip?"

"Yes, I talked to Mama."

"And what did she say?"

"She said, 'To love is to fear nothing.' I'm translating loosely from the Italian."

"She's right."

"I know, but . . . I'm not sure I love him."

"I felt the same way on my wedding day."

"You didn't have all this church hullabaloo."

"I know. But there was a reception. It was just as nerve-wracking."

"Steve . . . do you remember one night . . . I was six-teen, I think. You'd only been a cop a short time. Do you remember? I'd just come home from a date, and I was sitting in this room having some milk before I went to sleep. You must have had the four-to-midnight shift be-cause it was pretty late at night, and you were just coming in. You stopped in here and had milk with me. Do you remember?"

"Yes. I remember."

"Old Birnbaum's light was burning across the way. We could see it through the window there."

He looked across at the window and through it over the long expanse of his father's back yard to the gabled house belonging to Joseph Birnbaum, his father's closest friend and neighbor for forty years. He could remember that spring night clearly, the sound of insects in the back yard, the single light burning in Birnbaum's attic room, the thin yellow crescent of a moon hanging listlessly over the sharply slanting roof of the house.

"I told you what had happened to me that night," Angela said. "About . . . about the boy I'd dated and . . . what he'd tried to do."

"Yes, I remember"

"I never told Mama about that," Angela said. "You were the only one I ever told. And I asked you if this . . . happened all the time, if this was what I could expect from boys I dated. I wanted to know what to do, how I should behave. Do you remember what you told me?"

"Yes," Carella said.

"You said I should do whatever I felt was right. You said I would know what was right." She paused. "Steve . . . I've never . . ."

"Honey, shall I get Mama?"

"No, I want to talk to you. Steve, I don't know what to do tonight. I know that's awfully silly, I'm twenty-three years old, I should know what to do, but I don't, and I'm terrified he won't love me any more, he'll be disappointed, he'll . . ."

"Shhh, shhh," he said. "Come on now. What do you want?"

"I want you to tell me."

He looked into her eyes and he took her hands and said, "I can't do that, Slip."

"Why not?"

"Because you're not a baby in cotton slips any more, and you're not a little girl who's suddenly puzzled by her first kiss. You're a woman, Angela. And there isn't a man alive who can give a woman instructions about love. I don't think you'll need them, honey. I really don't think you'll need them."

"You think it'll . . . be all right?"

"I think it'll be fine. But I also think you'd better start dressing. Otherwise you'll miss your own wedding."

Angela nodded glumly.

"Come on," he said. "You're going to be the prettiest goddamn bride this neighborhood ever had." He hugged her, rose, and started for the door."

"Was . . . was Teddy frightened?" Angela asked.

"I'm going to give you one bit of brotherly advice," Carella said. "I won't tell you whether Teddy was frightened or puzzled or innocent or whatever. I won't tell you because marriage is a private thing, Angela, built on faith more than anything else. And whatever happens between you and Tommy—tonight or forever—you and he will be the only two people to ever know about it. And that's one of the frightening things about marriage . . . but it's also pretty damn reassuring." He went back to the bed, and he took her hands again, and he said, "Angela, you have nothing to worry about. He loves you so much he's trembling. He *loves* you, honey. He's a good man. You chose well."

"I love him, too, Steve. I do. Only . . ."

"Only *nothing*. What the hell do you want? A written guarantee that life is just a bowl of cherries? Well, it isn't. But you've got a clean slate, and you can write your own ticket. And, honey, you're starting with one of the major ingredients." He grinned. "You can't miss."

"Okay," she said, and she nodded her head emphatically.

"You going to get dressed?"

"Yes."

"Good."

"Okay," she said again, more emphatically. She paused. "But I think you're a louse for not giving me at least *one* hint!"

"I'm not a louse. I'm a loving brother."

"I feel better, Steve. Thank you."

"For what? Get dressed. Your blue garter is very pretty."

"Go to hell," she said, and he closed the door behind him, chuckling.

The boy's name was Ben Darcy.

He was twenty-six years old, with bright blue eyes and an engaging grin. He wore a blue mohair suit, and he walked across the back lawn with a long-legged lope, coming to a stop before the back porch where Tony Carella sat with his guests.

"Hello, Mr. Carella," he said. "Lots of activity going on. Are you excited?"

"The caterers," Tony said, looking out across the lawn at what seemed to be miles of white tablecloth. "You're early, Ben. The reception doesn't start until five."

"But the wedding's at three. You don't think I'd miss Angela's wedding, do you?"

"I think maybe she's gonna miss it herself," Tony said. "You know my daughter-in-law, Teddy? This is Ben Darcy."

"I think I've seen you before, Mrs. Carella," Ben said. Teddy nodded. Her back was killing her. She wanted to ask for a straight chair, but she knew Tony had given her the most comfortable chair on the porch, and she did not want to offend him.

"And these are some friends of my son," Tony said. "Miss Maxwell, Mr. Hawes, and Mr. Kling. Ben Darcy."

"Just call me Ben," Ben said, shaking hands all around. "I've known the Carellas so long I feel like a part of the family. Is there anything I can do to help, Mr. Carella?"

"Nothing. Just keep out of the way. For setting up those tables and things, they're making me a poor man." He wagged his head forlornly.

"He's the richest man on the block," Ben said, grinning. "Everybody in the neighborhood knows that."

"Sure, sure," Tony said.

"When we were kids, he used to give out free rolls at the back door of his bakery. But then he started pinching pennies. No more rolls." Ben shrugged.

"It was a free Salvation Army soup kitchen there," Tony said. "I figured out one day I was giving away five

hundred rolls a week to kids who come to the back door!
I also figured out it was the parents sending the kids
around to suck Tony Carella's blood. No more rolls!
Absolutely not! Cash on the line! No credit in my bakery!"

"He still gives away rolls," Ben said warmly. "All you
need is a hard-luck story, and Tony Carella begins weeping. If the story's good enough, he'll give you the whole
damn bake shop."

"Sure, sure. The Rockefeller Foundation, that's me.
I'm in business for my health."

Ben nodded, grinning. Idly, he asked, "Are you gentlemen in the baking line, too?"

Kling, ready to answer, glanced at Hawes first. Sitting
with the sunlight glowing in his red hair, the white streak
starkly naked against the flaming crimson, Hawes resembled nothing less than a baker. He caught Kling's eye and
said, "No, we're not bakers."

"That's right," Ben said. "You're friends of Steve,
aren't you?"

"Yes."

"Are you policemen?"

"Us?" Hawes said. He laughed convincingly. "Hell,
no."

Teddy and Christine looked at him curiously, but they
did not betray puzzlement.

"We're theatrical agents," Hawes lied unashamedly.
"Hawes and Kling, perhaps you've heard of us."

"No, I'm sorry."

"Yes," Hawes said. "Miss Maxwell is one of our
clients. She's going to be a big star one day, this girl."

"Oh, really?" Ben said. "What do you do, Miss Maxwell?"

"I . . ." Christine started, and then stopped.

"She's an exotic dancer," Hawes supplied, and Christine shot him an angry glare.

"An exot—?" Ben said.

"She strips," Hawes explained. "We've been trying to

convince Mr. Carella here to let Christine pop out of the wedding cake, but he doesn't think it's such a good idea."

Tony Carella laughed. Ben Darcy looked unconvinced.

"Hawes and Kling," Hawes repeated. "If you ever become interested in show business, give us a ring."

"I will," Ben said. "But I don't think I'll ever become interested in show business. I'm studying to be a dentist."

"That's a noble profession," Hawes said. "But it lacks the glamour of the entertainment world."

"Oh, teeth can be pretty exciting," Ben said.

"I'm sure," Hawes answered, "but what can compare to the fever pitch of opening night? Nothing! There's no business like show business."

"I guess you're right," Ben said, "but I'm glad I'm studying dentistry. I imagine I'll go into periodontal work later on." He paused. "It was Angela who first convinced me to become a professional man, you know."

"I didn't know," Hawes said.

"Oh yes. I used to date her. Date her? Hell, I began taking her out when she was seventeen and I guess I camped here on the Carella doorstep for the next five years. Wouldn't you say so, Mr. Carella?"

"Yes, he was a pest," Tony agreed.

"She's a wonderful girl," Ben said. "Tommy's a very lucky guy. There aren't many girls like Angela Carella around."

The screen door behind Ben clattered shut. He turned abruptly. Steve Carella came out onto the porch.

His father looked up. "She's all right?" he asked.

"She's all right," Carella said.

"Girls," Tony said mysteriously, and he shook his head.

"Hello, Ben," Carella said. "How are you?"

"Fine, thanks. You?"

"So-so. You're a little early, aren't you?"

"I guess so. I was just out for a walk, thought I'd stop by to see if I could lend a hand. Is Angela all right?"

"She's fine."

"Everything seems to be okay at Tommy's house. The limousine's there already."

"Oh?"

"Yep. Sitting in Tommy's driveway when I walked by there."

"Good. Then I better get started." He looked at his watch. "Honey, Bert and I will be riding with Tommy. You don't mind, do you?"

Teddy looked up at him. He could read in an instant any nuance on her mobile face. Deprived of speech since birth, her face had become a tool of expression so that meaning was instantly transmitted through her eyes and lips. He had expected displeasure at his announcement but, reading her face now, he saw only puzzlement and realized she had not "heard" him. Standing behind her as he'd spoken, he had not shown her his lips to read. He knelt beside her chair now.

"Bert and I are going to the church in Tommy's car. Is that all right with you?"

There was still no displeasure on her face. The puzzlement remained, and with it came a suspicious narrowing of the eyes. He knew in that moment that he had not fooled his wife. He had not told her of the incident with the black widow spider, but Teddy Carella—in her silent world—had already fathomed that something was amiss. The presence of Hawes and Kling was not the fulfillment of a social amenity. They were here as policemen, not wedding guests. She nodded, and then reached up to kiss him.

"I'll see you at the church," he said. "Are you all right?"

She nodded again. Her back was still killing her, but she sensed her husband had more important things on his mind than the trials of pregnancy. She flashed a sudden, radiant smile. Carella squeezed her hand.

"Come on, Bert," he said.

Chapter 4

A BLACK CADILLAC LIMOUSINE was parked in the driveway on the blind side of the Giordano house when Carella and Kling arrived. The car sat far back from the street, at the end of the concrete strips, close to the garage. The driver was nowhere in sight.

As they walked up onto the front porch, Kling said, "I make it for a gag, Steve. I think we're going to a lot of trouble for nothing."

"Well, maybe," Carella answered, and he rang the doorbell. "It doesn't hurt to be careful, though, does it?"

"I guess not. I get the feeling, however, that Cotton would much rather be elsewhere with his blonde." He paused. "But . . . that's show biz."

"Huh?" Carella said, and Tommy opened the door.

"Steve, hi! Come on in. I was just dressing. Do you know how to tie a bow tie? I've been trying for the past half-hour and getting nowhere. Come on in." He looked at Kling curiously.

"Bert Kling," Carella said, "Tommy Giordano, my future brother-in-law. Bert's with the squad, Tommy."

"Oh. Oh, yeah. Come on in. I feel pretty silly about all this, Steve. I think it's a gag."

Kling caught Carella's eye. "Well, gag or not," Carella said, "Bert and another friend of mine will be at the wedding and the reception."

"I appreciate what you're doing, Steve," Tommy said, "but in thinking it over, I'm pretty sure it was a gag. Come on into the bedroom, will you?"

39

They followed him through the house. In the bedroom, Tommy took a white tie from the dresser top and handed it to Carella. "Here," he said. "See what you can do with this damn thing, will you?"

He faced Carella. He lifted his chin, and Carella began working on the tie.

"I checked on Sokolin," Carella said.

"Yeah?"

"I don't want you to start worrying . . . but he's in this city. Got out of jail in April."

"Oh."

"Still think it's a gag?"

"Gee, I don't know. You think a guy would carry a grudge all this time? For something that happened in Korea? Or really, for something that didn't even . . ."

"Were you in Korea?" Kling asked, interested.

"Yeah. You?"

"Yeah."

"Army?"

"Yeah."

"I was in the Signal Corps," Tommy said. "With the Tenth Army Corps at the Inchon landings."

"I was in on the Seoul liberation," Kling said. "With the Ninth Corps."

"Under General Walker?"

"Yes."

"Hell, we linked up with the First and Ninth around Seoul!" Tommy said. "Jesus, I'll bet we were close enough to touch."

"You were on the drive to the Yalu?"

"Sure."

"How do you like that?" Kling said. "It's a small world, all right."

"And you're a cop now, huh?"

"Yes. What are you doing?"

"I work in a bank," Tommy said. "I'm training to be

an executive." He shrugged. "It's not really what I want to be."

"What do you want to be?"

"I'd like to be a baseball announcer. I used to be a pretty good catcher when I was a kid. I know the game inside out and backwards. Ask Jonesy when he gets back." He turned to Carella. "You didn't happen to see him downstairs, did you?"

"Who?" Carella said. "There. Your tie's tied."

"Jonesy. My best man. My best *friend,* too. He went downstairs about a half-hour ago, said he needed some air."

"Was he in a monkey suit?"

"Yeah."

"Didn't see anybody dressed for a wedding. Did you, Bert?"

"No."

"Well, he'll be back," Tommy said. "Jesus, I hope he has the ring. What time is it, Steve?"

"Two o'clock. You've still got an hour. Relax."

"Well, I'm supposed to get there a little earlier, you know. I've got to go back to the rectory. I'm not supposed to see the bride until she comes down the aisle. Your mother is a lulu, Steve."

"How so?"

"I'm not complaining. She'll probably make an excellent mother-in-law. But I called a little while ago, and she wouldn't even let me *talk* to Angela. That's going a little far, don't you think?"

"She was dressing," Carella said.

"Yeah?" Tommy's eyes glowed. "How does she look? Beautiful, I'll bet."

"Beautiful."

"Yeah, I knew it. Was she nervous?"

"Very."

"Me, too. You want some coffee?"

"No, thanks."

"A little drink?"

"No. Do you want to hear about Sokolin?"

"Sokolin? Who's—? Oh, sure. Sure." Tommy pulled on his jacket. "There. I'm all set. How do I look? Did I shave close enough?"

"You shaved close enough."

"I'll probably need another one by the time we check in tonight. I've got a heavy beard. You blond guys are lucky, Bert. Do I look all right, Steve? Is the tie straight?"

"The tie's straight."

"Good. Then I'm ready to go. You think we ought to leave now? It's past two, isn't it?"

"I think you ought to do something before you leave," Carella said.

"Yeah? What?"

"Put on your pants."

Tommy looked down at his hairy legs. "Oh, God! Oh, Jesus! Boy, am I glad you're here! How could a guy forget to do something he does every day of his life? Boy!" He shucked the jacket and took his black trousers from a hanger in the closet. "What about Sokolin?"

"He spent a year in jail because he got into an argument about his dead Korean buddy."

"That doesn't sound so good."

"It sounds pretty lousy. I don't imagine he's got much love in his heart for you."

A knock sounded at the front door. Tommy looked up and then slipped his suspenders over his shoulders. "Steve, would you get that, please? It's probably Jonesy."

Carella went to the front door and opened it. The boy standing there was about Tommy's age, twenty-six or twenty-seven. He wore his brown hair short. His gray eyes were alight with excitement. He looked very handsome in his tuxedo and his white starched shirt-front. Seeing Carella's similar uniform, he extended his hand and said, "Hi. Usher?"

"Nope. Relative," Carella said. He took the hand. "Steve Carella. Brother of the bride."

"Sam Jones. Best man. Call me Jonesy."

"Okay."

"How's our groom?"

"Nervous."

"Who isn't? I had to get out for a walk or I'd lose my mind." They went through the house into the bedroom. "You okay, Tommy?" Jonesy asked.

"I'm fine. I was ready to walk out of here without my pants, how do you like that?"

"Par for the course," Jonesy said.

"You've got dirt on your knees," Tommy said, looking down at his best man's trousers.

"What?" Jonesy followed his glance. "Oh, hell, I knew it. I tripped on the front step going out. Damn it!" He began brushing vigorously at his trousers.

"Do you have the ring?"

"Yep."

"Check."

"I've got it."

"Check anyway."

Jonesy stopped brushing his pants and stuck his forefinger into his vest pocket. "It's there. Ready for delivery. Jones to Giordano."

"Jonesy used to pitch on our team," Tommy said. "I caught. I already told you that, didn't I?"

"Jones to Giordano," Jonesy said again. "He was a damn good catcher."

"You did all the work," Tommy said, zipping up his fly. "There. Now for the jacket. Have I got my shoes on?" He looked down at his feet.

"He was like this before every game," Jonesy said, grinning. "I know this guy since he was three years old, would you believe it?"

"We used to get walked around the park together," Tommy said. "Jonesy missed the Korean bit because he's got a trick knee. Otherwise we'd have been in that together, too."

"He's the meanest bastard ever walked the earth," Jonesy said playfully. "I don't know why I like him."

"Yok-yok," Tommy said. "We've got mutual wills, Steve, did you know that?"

"What do you mean?"

"Had them drawn up when I got out of the service. Birnbaum's son made them out for us. Birnbaum and his wife witnessed them. Remember, Jonesy?"

"Sure. But you'd better have yours changed now. You're gonna be a married man in a few hours."

"That's right," Tommy said.

"What do you mean, mutual wills?" Carella asked.

"Our wills. They're identical. Jonesy gets everything I own if I die, and I get everything he owns if he dies."

Jonesy shrugged. "You'll have to change that now," he said.

"Sure, I will. When we get back from the honeymoon. But I never regretted the wills, did you?"

"No, *sir*."

"Birnbaum thought we were both nuts, remember? Wanted to know why two such young fellows were making out wills. His wife—may she rest in peace—kept clucking her tongue all the while she signed. What ever happened to that lawyer son of his, anyway?"

"He's out West now. Denver or someplace. He's got a big practice out there."

"Poor Birnbaum. All alone here in the city." Tommy stood at attention, ready for inspection. "Pants on, tie tied, shoes shined. Am I okay now?"

"You're beautiful," Jonesy said.

"Then let's go. Ooops, cigarettes." He snatched a package from the dresser. "Have you got the ring?"

"I've got it."

"Check again."

Jonesy checked again. "It's still there."

"Okay, let's go. What time is it?"

"Two-twenty," Carella said.

"Good. We'll be a little early, but that's good. Let's go."

They went out of the house. Tommy locked the door behind him, and then turned left, walking toward the driveway lined with tall poplars which shielded it from the house next door. They walked toward the car with all the solemnity of a funeral party.

"Where's the driver?" Tommy asked.

"I told him he could go get a cup of coffee," Jonesy said. "He should be back by now."

"Here he comes," Kling said.

They watched the driver as he ambled up the street. He was a short man wearing the black uniform and peaked cap of a rental service. "Ready to go?" he asked.

"We're ready," Tommy said. "Where were you?"

"Up the street getting a cup of coffee." The driver looked offended. "Your best man said it was all right."

"Okay, okay, let's go," Tommy said.

They got into the limousine, and the driver began backing into the street.

"Wait a minute," Tommy said. The driver turned. "What's that?"

"What?"

"There. In the driveway. Where we just came from."

"I don't see anything."

"Have you got the ring, Jonesy?"

Jonesy felt in his pocket. "Yes, I've got it."

"Oh. Okay. I thought I saw something glinting on the concrete. Okay, let's go. Let's go."

The driver backed out of the driveway and turned into the street.

"Relax," Jonesy said.

"Boy, I wish I could."

The limousine moved slowly up the tree-lined street.

The sun was shining in an eggshell blue sky. It was a beautiful day.

"Can't you go any faster?" Tommy asked.

"We've got plenty of time," the driver said.

He stopped at an intersection at the top of a long hill. Patiently, he waited for the light to change.

"You turn left at the bottom of the hill," Tommy said. "The church is on the left."

"I know."

"Oh, hell," Jonesy said suddenly.

"Huh?"

"Cigarettes! I forgot cigarettes."

"I've got some," Tommy said.

"I'll need my own." He opened the door on his side. "I'll get some at the candy store. Go ahead without me before you bust a gut. I'll walk down the hill." He slammed the door behind him and started for the sidewalk.

"Don't get lost!" Tommy yelled after him frantically.

"I won't. Don't worry." He vanished inside the candy store on the corner.

"The light's green," Tommy said. "Go ahead."

The driver put the car into gear and started down the hill. It was a long steep hill with one street bisecting it. It ran at a sharp pitch to a second street at the far end, a dead end blocked by a stone wall which shielded a steep-angled cliff of jagged rock. The stone wall was painted with alternating yellow and black lines as a warning to approaching motorists. As a further precaution, a huge blinking DEAD END sign flashed in the exact center of the wall. Since the time that excavation for gravel had begun in the area behind the wall, leaving the rocky cliff and the steep drop, only one motorist had driven through the wall and over the cliff. He'd been killed instantly, and it was learned later that he'd been drunk, but the accident had been enough to warrant the yellow-and-black paint job and the blinking light.

The limousine gained momentum as the car hurtled toward the end of the hill and the painted stone wall.

"That's a bad turn at the corner," Tommy said. "Be careful."

"Mister, I've been driving for twenty years," the driver said. "I never missed a wedding yet, and I never yet had an accident."

"Yeah, well there's a steep cliff behind that wall. A guy was killed here once."

"I know all about it. Don't worry, you ain't gonna get killed. When you been married for fifteen years, the way I have, you'll maybe wish you *did* get into an accident on your wedding day."

The car sped for the bottom of the hill and the turn. The DEAD END sign blinked monotonously. Clutching the wheel in two massive fists, the driver swung it sharply to the left.

There was an enormous cracking sound which jolted the automobile.

The car did not turn to the left.

With something like awe in his voice, the driver said, "Jesus, it won't steer!"

Chapter 5

FROM OUTSIDE THE CAR, passers-by saw only a vehicle which was wildly out of control, the front wheels pointing in opposite directions as the limousine hurtled forward toward the sidewalk, the stone wall, and the cliff beyond.

Inside the car, the passengers only knew that the driver could not, for some reason, steer the limousine. In a last desperate effort, he swung the steering wheel to the right and then the left, his foot automatically leaping to the brake pedal. The car swung in a screeching arc toward the sidewalk, its back wheels leaping the curb, the rear end swinging toward the wall and the cliff.

"Brace yourself!" Carella shouted, and the men in the car tensed for the shock of impact, surprised when the shock was not as great as they expected, startled with the knowledge that something had intervened to prevent the powerful smash through the stone wall, amazed when they realized the something was a lamppost.

The car ricocheted off the unbending steel pole, swerved in another wild arc, bounced forward onto the front wheels finally, coming to a dead stop as the brakes took hold completely and irrevocably.

The men in the automobile were silent.

The driver was the first to speak.

He said only, "Wow!"

One by one, they climbed out of the car. Kling had banged his head on the roof of the car, but otherwise no one was injured. The car itself had fared worse. The entire right side was smashed in where the limousine had collided with the lamppost. A crowd was gathering on the sidewalk. A policeman began shoving his way through it. The driver of the Cadillac began talking to him, explaining what had happened.

Carella walked to the steel lamppost and slapped it with an open hand. "We can all get down on our hands and knees and kiss this baby," he said. "If it hadn't stopped us—" He looked over the stone wall, and then wiped his forehead.

"What the hell do you suppose happened?" Kling asked.

"I don't know," Carella said. "Come on."

Together, they walked to where the driver and the patrolman were squatting on their hands and knees at the front of the car.

They waited.

"Sure," the driver said to the cop. "That's it."

"Yeah," the cop said. "Boy, you were lucky you hit that lamppost. A guy was killed here once, you know that?"

"What is it?" Carella asked.

"The steering linkage," the driver said. "There's a steering tube under there, connected to the tie rod ends. Well, the one on the right side busted. And without that tie rod end, I didn't have any control."

"It looks like more than that," the patrolman said.

"What does it look like?" Carella asked.

"It looks like somebody worked on that thing with a hack saw!"

At 3:30 P.M., Tommy Giordano and his best man stepped from the rectory of the Church of the Sacred Heart and walked to the altar. In a loud stage whisper, Tommy asked, "Have you got the ring?" and Jonesy nodded in assurance.

Angela Carella, resplendent in white, entered the back of the church on her father's arm. Her face beneath the white veil was frozen in lovely horror.

On one side of the church, sitting with the bride's family, were Steve and Teddy Carella, and Bert Kling. On the other side, sitting with the groom's relatives, were Cotton Hawes and Christine Maxwell. Organ music filled the vaulted stone vastnesses of the church. A photographer who'd snapped Angela as she'd stepped out of the Cadillac, snapped her again as she'd mounted the church steps, and again as she'd started down the aisle, now hopped with gnomelike agility to the front of the church, anxious to catch her as she approached the altar. Tommy's hands twitched at his sides.

Louisa Carella began crying. Teddy reached over to pat her mother-in-law's hand, and then reached for her own handkerchief, and blew her nose to hide her tears.

"She's beautiful," Louisa said, and Teddy nodded, her eyes brimming.

The organ music swelled to drown out the sound of the joyful weeping, the "Ooooohs" and "Ahhhhs" which heralded the bride's steady regal progress down the aisle. The flash bulbs popped as the photographer busily kept his shutter clicking. Tony Carella, his bent arm supporting the trembling hand of his daughter, walked down the aisle with the dignity of a monarch about to be crowned, certain that the twitching of his left eye was not visible to anyone in the pews.

In the first pew on the bride's half of the church, Steve Carella sat alongside his wife and chewed his lip.

Somebody sawed through that rod end, he thought. *This was no damn black widow joke. This was serious business.*

Angela climbed the steps to the altar. Tommy smiled at her, and she returned the smile, and then lowered her eyes behind the pale white veil.

And whoever did the sawing was well aware of that steep hill and that sharp turn. Whoever did it probably sawed it through just far enough to know it would snap when the turn was attempted.

Tony Carella handed his daughter to his soon-to-be-son. Together, the couple faced the priest. The church was still with the solemnity of the occasion.

Tommy saw something glinting on the driveway as we pulled out, Carella thought. *Probably metal filings from the sawed rod. The rod is thin. Ten minutes with a hack saw could have done a very fine job on it. And Sam Jones was gone for a half-hour walk. And Sam Jones had dirt on the knees of his trousers. And it was Sam Jones who gave the driver permission to leave the limousine in search of a cup of coffee.*

The priest said a prayer and then blessed the couple with holy water. Tommy was sweating profusely. Beneath the white veil, Angela's lips were trembling.

"Do you, Thomas Giordano," the priest said, "take this woman as your lawfully wedded wife to live together in the state of holy matrimony? Will you love, honor and keep her as a faithful man is bound to do, in health, sickness, prosperity, and adversity, and forsaking all others keep you alone unto her 'til death do you part?"

Tommy swallowed hard. "Yes," he said. "I do."

"Do you, Angela Louisa Carella, take this man as your lawfully wedded husband to live together in the state of holy matrimony? Will you love, honor and cherish him as a faithful woman is bound to do, in health, sickness . . ."

And it was Sam Jones, Carella thought, *who conveniently stepped out of the automobile to buy a package of cigarettes just before the crash.*

". . . prosperity and adversity, and forsaking all others keep you alone unto him 'til death do you part?"

"I do," Angela whispered.

It is also Sam Jones, best man and best friend, who is named in Tommy's will, who gets everything Tommy owns should Tommy die. Sam Jones.

"For as you have both consented in wedlock and have acknowledged it before God and this company, I do by virtue of the authority vested in me by the Catholic Church and the laws of this state now pronounce you husband and wife."

The priest made the sign of the cross over the young couple and, sobbing next to Teddy, Louisa Carella suddenly said, "Now I have *another* married daughter," and she took Teddy's hand and kissed it quickly and fervently.

Tommy lifted his bride's veil and kissed her fleetingly and with much embarrassment. The organ music started again. Smiling, the veil pulled back onto the white crown nestled in her hair, Angela clutched Tommy's arm and they started up the aisle, the photographer recording every inch of their progress.

In the rectory, the telephone began ringing.

The nun in the rectory held the door open for Steve Carella as he stepped into the small room. Standing by the telephone in the robes he'd worn during the ceremony, Father Paul said, "I knew it'd take a wedding to get you into the church, Steve. But I didn't guess a phone call would bring you into the rectory."

"Two things I never discuss are politics and religion," Carella answered. "Is the call from the squad, Father?"

"A man named Meyer Meyer," Father Paul said.

"Thank you," Carella said, and he took the receiver from the priest's hand. "Hello, Meyer. Steve."

"Hello, boy. How goes the wedding?"

"So far, so good. The knot's been tied."

"I've been doing a little further checking on this Sokolin character. Are you still interested?"

"Very much so."

"Okay. I checked with his parole officer. He's been leading an exemplary life, working as a salesman in a department store downtown. But two weeks ago, he moved from Isola to Riverhead. I've got the address, Steve. From what the map tells me, it looks as if it's eleven blocks from your father's house."

Carella thought for a moment and then said, "Meyer, will you do me a favor? We had an accident a little while ago that stank to high heaven. Will you put a pickup-and-hold on this character? I'd feel a hell of a lot safer." He suddenly remembered he was in a church rectory and glanced sheepishly at Father Paul.

"Sure thing. It's kind of slow around here, anyway. I may go out on it myself."

"Will you let me know when you've got him? We're heading for the photographer's right now, but I'll be at my father's place in about an hour. You can reach me there."

"Right. Kiss the bride for me, will you?"

"I will. Thanks again, Meyer." He hung up.

Father Paul looked at him and said, "Trouble?"

"No. Nothing serious."

"I've been told about the automobile accident," he said. "Quite a freak occurrence."

"Yes."

"But there's no trouble?"

"No."

"Even though the accident, to quote you, stank to high heaven?"

Carella smiled. "Father," he said, "you've got me inside the church, but you're not going to get me into the confessional." He shook hands with the priest. "It was a beautiful ceremony. Thank you, Father."

Outside, the limousines were waiting.

Carella walked over to where Kling was standing with Teddy.

"That was Meyer," he said. "I've got a pickup-and-hold on Sokolin. I think that's wise, don't you?"

"I suppose."

Carella looked around. "Where's our friend Jonesy?"

"He went back to the house."

"Oh."

"If you're thinking what I'm thinking, don't worry about it. Cotton left right after him."

"Good." He took Teddy's arm. "Honey, you look about ready to drop. Come on. Get inside that nice air-cooled Cadillac." He held the door open for her. "Some day," he said, "when I get to be commissioner, I'm going to buy you one of these all for yourself."

Ben Darcy and Sam Jones were talking to the caterers when Hawes and Christine pulled up in a taxicab. Hawes paid the driver, and then walked around to the back of the Carella house. A huge framework was in its last stages of construction at the far end of the plot, just inside the row of hedges which divided the Carella property from Birnbaum's.

Jonesy stopped talking when he saw Christine Maxwell. Wearing an ice-blue chiffon, she rustled across the lawn clinging to Hawes's arm, and Jonesy followed her progress through the grass with unabashed and open admiration. When they were close enough, his eyes still on Christine, he said, "I don't believe we've met. My name is Sam Jones. Call me Jonesy."

"I'm Cotton Hawes," Hawes said. "This is Christine Maxwell."

"Pleased to meet you," he said, taking Christine's hand. Belatedly, he added, "Both."

"What's this monster creation?" Hawes asked, indicating the huge wooden grid.

"For the fireworks display," one of the caterers explained.

"It looks like the launching platform for a three-stage rocket," Hawes commented, aware of the sledgehammer subtlety of Jonesy's ogling and slightly rankled by it. "Are we trying for the moon?"

"We'll be shooting off a few rockets," the caterer replied humorlessly.

"When will this be?"

"As soon as it's dark. This is going to be the goddamnedest wedding *this* neighborhood ever saw, you can bet on that."

"Angela deserves it," Darcy said.

"And Tommy, too," Jonesy added, smiling at Christine. "Have you seen the mermaid, Miss Maxwell? Come, I'll show it to you. They've already loaded the buckets of champagne. It's fascinating."

"Well . . ." Christine started, and she glanced hesitantly at Hawes.

"I'm sure Mr. Hawes won't mind," Jonesy said. "Come along." He took her arm and led her to where the ice maiden lay on her side, protected from the sun by a shielding canopy. The base upon which she lay had been scooped out to form a frigid tub into which dozens of champagne bottles had been placed. It truly looked as if this was going to be one hell of a wedding. Hawes watched Christine amble away across the lawn, aware of a growing irritation within him. It was one thing to do a cotton-picking, bodyguarding favor, but it was another to have a girl snatched from right before your eyes.

"So what is this?" a voice beside him said. "The battleship *Missouri?*"

Hawes turned. The man standing before the fireworks scaffolding was short and slender with a balding pate fringed with white hair. His blue eyes held a merry twinkle. He studied the framework as if it were truly a wonder of the scientific age.

"I'm Birnbaum," he said. "The neighbor. Who are you?"

"Cotton Hawes."

They shook hands. "That's an unusual name," Birnbaum said. "Very unusual. Cotton Mather? The Puritan priest?"

"Yes."

"I'm not a religious man, myself."

"Neither am I."

"Did you come from the wedding?"

"Yes," Hawes said.

"Me, too. It was the first time in my life I've ever been inside a Catholic Church. I'll tell you something. It's a *bubemeiseh.*"

"What is?"

"That the walls will fall down if a Jew steps inside. I stepped inside and I stepped out again, and the walls—thank God—are still standing. Imagine if the walls had come down during my *tsotskuluh's* wedding. A terrible thing to imagine! *Oi,* God, I would rather cut off my right arm. She looked lovely, didn't she?"

"Yes."

"A beautiful girl, Angela. I never had a daughter. I got a lawyer son, he's now in Denver. My wife, poor soul, passed away three years ago. I'm alone in the world. Birnbaum. The neighbor. Well, at least I'm a neighbor, no?"

"A neighbor is a good thing to be," Hawes said, smiling, liking the little man immensely.

"Certainly. But lest you think I'm a bum, I should tell you I am also a grocery store owner besides being a neighbor. Birnbaum's Grocery. Right up the street. And I live over there. See the house? Been here for forty years and believe me when I first moved in people thought Jews had horns and tails. Well, times change, huh? It's a good thing, thank God." He paused. "I know both the children since they were born. Tommy and Angela. Like my own children. Both sweet. I love that little girl. I never had a daughter of my own, you know. So Tony's having fireworks! My God, what a wedding this will be! I hope I live through it. Do you like my tuxedo?"

"It's very nice," Hawes said.

"The least I could do was rent a tuxedo when Tony's daughter got married. It fits a little snug, don't you think?"

"No, it looks fine."

"Well, I'm not as slender as I used to be. Too much easy living. I got two clerks in my grocery store now. It's not easy to buck the supermarkets. But I get by. Get by? Look how fat I'm getting. What do you do for a living?"

"I'm a theatrical agent," Hawes said, relying upon the earlier fabrication. If someone meant to injure Tommy Giordano, he did not think it wise to advertise his profession.

"That's a good business. Is Miss Maxwell in show business?"

"Yes," he lied again. "She's a dancer."

"I thought so. A beautiful girl. But I'm partial to blondes." He looked across the lawn. "I guess Jonesy isn't. He's left her."

Hawes turned. Christine was walking back toward the fireworks platform. Alone. Jonesy was nowhere in sight.

It suddenly occurred to him that Ben Darcy had disappeared, too.

I'm a fine cop, Hawes thought. *I stand here talking to a grocer while the boys I'm supposed to watch vanish into the woodwork.*

"You should take a look at the mermaid," Christine said. "She's quite lovely."

"Where'd your escort go?" Hawes asked.

Christine shrugged. "Said there was something he had to take care of." She paused. "I didn't inquire further. I didn't think it would be ladylike." She paused again. "He's rather cute, don't you think?"

"Adorable," Hawes said, and he wondered where both Jonesy and Darcy had gone.

And he hoped it was not too far.

Chapter 6

THE PHOTOGRAPHER'S SHOP was not too far from the Carella house in Riverhead. In fact, a fairly slow driver could make the journey in less than five minutes if he stopped at each FULL STOP sign on the way.

The photographer was called Jody Lewis, and a sign across the front of his shop read JODY'S simply because he did not wish to name his place LEWIS'S or LEWIS', both of which he was certain would be mistakenly read as just plain LEWIS. The shop was a simple one-story brick building with a plate-glass front window behind which were displayed the photographer's previous efforts. Across the street from the shop, sitting back some twenty-five feet from the sidewalk, was a two-story frame house. Six windows faced the street side of that house. From a window on the second floor of the house, the photographer's shop was clearly visible.

The man stood at the window, peering across the street at the shop. The cars had not yet arrived. That was good. That gave him plenty of time to set up. He lighted a cigar and then crossed the room to where the rifle was standing against the wall.

The rifle was a Winchester Model 70 target rifle which had been developed to meet the requirements of all long-range, high-power target shooting, and long-range shooting at small game. The stock was ample in size and weight, with a large butt stock, a well-rounded comb, and a large full pistol grip curving close to the guard. The gun also featured a target butt plate and a long, wide beavertail forestock.

He picked up the gun and studied it, the cigar smoke trailing up past his face.

A telescopic sight was mounted to the gun.

The sight was a blued steel tube, one inch in diameter, eleven and a quarter inches in length. It weighed only nine and a half ounces and was adjustable for internal windage and elevation with either a friction lock or a quarter-inch click.

The man carried the gun to the window and rested it on the window sill. He focused the sight on the door of Jody's shop, so that the crosshairs were on the center of the doorway.

Then he sat back to wait.

The two limousines pulled up before he'd been waiting five minutes.

He pulled back the bolt and slammed it home, rested the gun on the window sill again, and took careful aim at the entrance to the shop. He looked up from the sight once to make sure he knew which of the people coming from the cars was Tommy Giordano.

Then he waited again.

Tommy stepped into the door of the shop.

The man's finger began to tighten on the trigger. And then Tommy pulled his bride to him, her back to the street, kissing her soundly. The finger hesitated. Tommy pulled her into the shop. The moment was gone.

Cursing, the sniper stubbed out his cigar and prepared to wait for their exit.

Jody Lewis was a dwarf of a man who looked like something which had popped out of a trick box camera when the shutter was clicked. Bouncing around his shop with undiminished energy, he said, "These are the only posed pictures we'll take. Of the bride and groom. This is your story, the bride's and groom's. That's why I don't want any posed shots of the best man or the maid of honor. Who needs them? This is your story. That's what it'll say on the cover of the album. 'Our Wedding Day.' Not the best man's wedding day, but the groom's. Not the maid of honor's, but the bride's. And all I want here in the studio with the good lights is one perfect picture of the lovely bride, God bless her, and one perfect picture of the handsome groom, and one of you together. And that's all. And then we go off to the reception. But is that the end of Jody Lewis? Not by a long shot. Not by a closeup, either. I'll be with you every minute of the way, taking pictures of you when you least expect it. Click, click, click goes my shutter. A candid record of your wedding day. Right to the hotel, right to a shot of Tommy carrying you over the threshold, and you putting your shoes in the hallway. And then back to develop and print, so that when you return from your lovely honeymoon, you'll have this candid album titled 'Our Wedding Day' as a keepsake forever, as a memento of events you might otherwise forget. Who can remember all the little things that have happened or are going to happen today? Nobody has a memory like that except a camera. And I am a camera! Me, Jody Lewis, from the play and movie of the same name.

Now sit right here, little ones. The two of you together.
That's it. Look as if you love each other, I'm joking, God
only knows you're crazy in love with each other, that's it,
smile a little, Tommy, my God, don't look so serious, the
girl loves you. That's better. Take his hand, Angela.
That's the girl, now look over there, not at the camera,
over there where the picture's hanging on the wall, that's
it, hold it, click! That's going to be beautiful. Now turn a
little on the seat, Tommy, that's it, and put your arms
around her waist, oh she's nice to hold, my friend, that's
it, don't blush, you're married now, that's it, now hold it,
hold it . . ."

"How do you feel, Teddy?" Carella asked.

Gently, Teddy touched the mound which began just
below her breasts. Then she rolled her eyes heavenward
and pulled a weary face.

"It'll be over soon," he said. "Is there anything you
want? A glass of water or something?"

Teddy shook her head.

"Massage your back?"

She shook her head again.

"Know I love you?"

Teddy grinned and squeezed his hand.

The woman who answered the door at the private
house in Riverhead was in her late fifties and didn't care.
She wore a wrinkled housedress and scuffed house-slip-
pers. Her hair hung limply on her head, as if it had followed its owner's directive and given up the struggle.

"What do you want?" she said. She pierced Meyer
and O'Brien with eyes chipped from green agate.

"We're looking for a man named Marty Sokolin,"
Meyer said patiently. "Does he live here?"

"Yes, and who the hell are you?"

Patiently, Meyer took out his wallet and opened it to
where his shield was pinned to the leather. "Police department," he said.

The woman looked at the shield. "All right, Mr. Detective," she said. "What did Sokolin do?"

"Nothing. We just want to ask him a few questions."

"What about?"

"About what he might be planning to do."

"He ain't here," the woman said.

"And what is your name, madam?" Meyer asked patiently. If there was one attribute Meyer possessed, it was extreme patience. An Orthodox Jew born in a predominantly Gentile neighborhood, he'd been further handicapped by the vagaries of a whimsical father who thought it would be a good joke to give his son a double-barreled monicker. The family surname was Meyer. And old Max Meyer decided to name his change-of-life offspring Meyer Meyer, just to get even with the powers that dictated off-season births. The joke was played. It was not a very practical one. It provided the young boy with a ready-made millstone. To say that Meyer Meyer's childhood had been only an endless round of fist fights provoked by either his name or his religion would have been a complete understatement. For coupled with the fist fights came the slow development of a diplomat. Meyer learned that only *some* battles could be won with his hands. The rest had to be won with his tongue. And so he acquired a veneer of extreme patience to cover the scars of his father's little jibe. Patiently, he even learned to forgive the old man before he died. Now, at the age of thirty-seven, the only scar he carried from an excruciatingly anxious childhood (or, to be more precise, the only scar which *showed*) was a head as bald as the famed American eagle.

Patiently, he repeated, "And what is your name, madam?"

"Mary Murdoch. What's it to you?"

"Nothing," Meyer said. He glanced at O'Brien. O'Brien stepped back a pace, as if anxious to sever whatever national ties bound him to the woman. "You said Mr. Sokolin was not in. When did he leave, might we ask?"

"Early this morning. He took his damn horn with him, thank the good Lord."

"His horn?"

"His trumpet, his trombone, his saxophone, whatever you call the damn thing. He practices it morning and night. You never heard such unholy screeches. I wouldn't have rented him the apartment if I'd known he played a horn. I might kick him out, matter of fact."

"You don't like horn players?"

"Put it this way," Mary Murdoch said. "They make me vomit."

"That's a unique way of putting it," Meyer said, and he cleared his throat. "How do you know Sokolin left with his horn?"

"I seen him. He's got a case for the thing. A black case. That's what he carries the damn thing in. A case."

"A trumpet case?"

"Or a trombone, or a saxophone, some damn thing. It sure makes an unholy racket, whatever it is."

"How long has he been living here, Miss Murdoch?"

"*Mrs.* Murdoch, if you please. He's been living here for two weeks. If he keeps blasting away on that damn saxophone, he won't be living here much longer, I can tell you that."

"Oh, is it a saxophone?"

"Or a trumpet, or a trombone, or some damn thing," she said. "Is he in trouble with the police?"

"No, not really. Do you have any idea where he went when he left this morning?"

"No. He didn't say. I just happened to see him go, that's all. But he usually hangs out in a bar on the Avenue."

"What avenue is that, Mrs. Murdoch?"

"Dover Plains Avenue. Everybody knows the Avenue Don't you know the Avenue?"

"No, we're not too familiar . . ."

"Two blocks down and under the elevated structure.

Dover Plains Avenue. Everybody knows the Avenue. He hangs out in a bar there. It's called the Easy Dragon, that's some name for a bar, isn't it? It sounds more like a Chinese restaurant." Mrs. Murdoch grinned with death's head simplicity.

"You're sure he hangs out there?"

"Sure, I'm sure."

"How can you be sure?"

"Put it this way," Mrs. Murdoch said. "I'm not above taking a little nip every now and then myself."

"I see."

"Which don't make me a drunkard."

"I know."

"All right. You finished?"

"I guess so. We may be back."

"What for?"

"You're so pleasant to talk to," Meyer said, and Mrs. Murdoch slammed the door.

"Well!" O'Brien said.

"Luckily, she didn't start shooting," Meyer said. "With you along, I always expect bullets."

"Maybe she'll shoot when we come back. *If* we come back."

"Maybe so. Keep your fingers crossed."

"Where to now?"

"The Easy Dragon," Meyer said. "Where else?"

The Easy Dragon was named the Easy Dragon for no apparent reason. The decor was not Chinese. There was not a Chinese in sight anywhere. The Easy Dragon looked like any tavern in any suburban neighborhood, peopled with the usual sprinkling of Sunday afternoon drinkers. Meyer and O'Brien entered the place, adjusted their vision to the dimness after the brilliant sunshine outside, and walked to the bar.

Meyer flashed the tin instantly. The bartender studied his shield with great dispassion.

"So?" he said.

"We're looking for a guy named Marty Sokolin. Know him?"

"So?"

"Yes or no?"

"Yes. So?"

"Is he here now?"

"Don't you know what he looks like?"

"No. Is he here?"

"No. What'd he do?"

"Nothing. Are you expecting him today?"

"Who knows? He's in and out. He's only been living in the neighborhood a short time. What'd he do?"

"I told you. Nothing."

"Is he a little crazy?"

"How do you mean?"

"You know. A little crazy." The bartender circled his temple with an extended forefinger. "Cuckoo."

"What makes you think he's crazy?"

"He's got a fanatical gleam in his eyes. Especially when he's drinking. Also, he's a big bastard. I wouldn't want to ever tangle with him. This guy chews railroad spikes and spits out carpet tacks." He paused. "Pardon the cliché," he said. He pronounced it "cleesh."

"You're pardoned. Do you happen to know where he might be right now?"

"You tried his house?"

"Yes."

"He ain't there, huh?"

"No."

"What'd he do?"

"Nothing. Would you mind, if you know, telling us where he might be?"

"Well, I'm not sure I know. You tried his girl's pad?"

"No. Who's she?"

"A dame named Oona. Oona I don't know what. How's

that for a fancy name? You should see her. She's like a regular bombshell. Perfect for a nut like Sokolin."

"Oona, huh? And you don't know her last name."

"That's right. Just Oona. You won't miss her if you see her. She's a blonde with bazooms like pineapples." He paused. "Pardon the cliché," he said.

"You're pardoned. Any idea where she lives?"

"Sure."

"Where?"

"Up the street. There's a rooming house on the corner. She's new around here, too. The only reason I know where she lives is she mentioned she was at a place served meals. And the place on the corner is the only place serves meals. I mean, of the rooming houses."

"I see," Meyer said. "Can you describe her a little more fully?"

"Well, like I said, she's got these enormous pineapples. And she's got a mouth like a trap, and a pretty nose, and eyes like blue ice and blond hair like a field of wheat." He paused, retracing the path of his similes to see if he'd been guilty of another "cleesh." Apparently satisfied of his innocence, he nodded and said, "If you find her, you can't miss her."

"That's reassuring," Meyer said. "Has she been in today?"

"No."

"Did Sokolin ever play a horn in here?"

"A what?"

"A horn."

"No. He plays a horn, does he? Boy, miracles will never cease."

"What's the name of this rooming house? Where they serve meals?"

"The Green Corner." He shrugged. "The house is green, and it's on the corner. Listen, who knows why people name places?"

"Is this your place?" Meyer asked.

"Yeah."

"Why'd *you* name it the Easy Dragon?"

"Oh, that was a mistake. The sign painter misunderstood me on the telephone. So after all the signs were painted, I figured why bother changing it to what I wanted originally?"

"What had you wanted originally?"

"The place was supposed to be called the Easy Drag Inn." He shrugged. "Listen, people goof all the time. That's why they've got erasers on penc—" and he stopped himself before uttering the banality.

"Well, come on, Bob," Meyer said. "Thanks a lot for your time, mister."

"Not at all. Think you'll get her?"

"All we want to do is get *him*," Meyer said.

All I want to do, the sniper thought, *is get him.*

What's taking them so long in there? How many pictures do they have to snap, anyway?

He looked at his watch.

They had been inside the shop for forty minutes already. Weren't they due back at the house? Shouldn't the reception be starting any minute? For God's sake, what was taking them so long?

The front door of the shop opened.

The sniper peered through the telescopic sight of the rifle, fixing the doorway smack on the intersection of the crosshairs.

He waited.

One by one, the wedding party began pouring through the open door of the shop.

Where the hell was Tommy Giordano?

Was that . . . ? No. Not him.

There now, there's the bride . . . there's . . .

Tommy appeared in the doorway. The sniper held his breath.

One, two . . . now!

He squeezed the trigger, pulling off two shots in rapid succession.

From the street, the shots sounded like the backfire of an automobile. Already inside one of the limousines, Carella didn't even hear them. Both slugs struck the brick wall to the left of the doorjamb and then ricocheted into the air, spent. Tommy, unaware, ran to the first car and climbed in with his bride.

The sniper cursed as the cars pulled away.

Then he packed his rifle.

Chapter 7

AT ONE END of Tony Carella's lot, close to the Carella-Birnbaum property line and to the left of the fireworks stage, Weddings–Fetes, Incorporated, had constructed a bandstand. Hung with white bunting, adorned with flowers, it provided a magnificent setting for the local band Tony had hired. The band was called the Sal Martino Orchestra. The band—or the "orchestra" as Sal preferred to call it—consisted of:

> One piano player
> One drummer
> Four saxophonists (two tenor men and two
> alto men)
> Two trumpeters (one lead trumpeter and
> one second-trumpeter)
> And a trombonist

Actually, the ensemble would have been complete—
oh, sure, the rhythm section *could* have used a bass
player, but why be picky—would have been complete
without the trombonist. A two-man brass section in an
eight-piece band (orchestra, that is) was certainly enough
brass power. The lead trumpeter would carry the section,
and the second trumpeter would handle all the hot solos
and screech work. Since the band (orchestra, of course)
had a full sax section each member of which doubled on
clarinet, the two trumpets would have afforded a well-
balanced complement of brass. There really was no need
for the trombone.

Sal Martino played the trombone.

He also played the French horn, but never on jobs.
He restricted his French horning to the privacy of his
bedroom. In all fairness, he was not a bad French horn-
ist, nor was he a bad trombonist. It was just that the band
needed him the way they needed a flatted fifth. Or an
augmented seventh. The band preferred their chords to be
simple and major. A diminished ninth could throw their
rehearsals into a tizzy for a solid week. Simplicity was
the keynote of the Sal Martino Orchestra. And simplicity
certainly did not call for a trombonist in the brass section.
But such are the vagaries of leadership.

Besides, Sal Martino looked like a real pro when he
was up there leading the band. He was a man in his late
twenties, with a high crown of black hair and a small
black mustache. His eyes were blue and very soulful. He
had broad shoulders and a narrow waist and long legs
which he wobbled with Presley-like ease while conducting.
He sometimes conducted with his right hand. He sometimes conducted with the end of his trombone. He sometimes simply smiled out at the crowd and didn't conduct
at all. Whichever way he did it, the band sounded the
same.

Lousy.

Well, not lousy. But pretty bad.

They sounded especially bad when they were tuning up, but then all bands sound bad when they are taking their *A* from the piano player. At 4:45 that afternoon, the Martino Orchestra was warming up and tuning up and sounding very much like the Boston Pops Symphony minus the Boston and minus the Symphony. Hawes, a music lover by nature, could barely sit still as he listened to the cacophony. He was also slightly disturbed by the fact that neither Sam Jones nor Ben Darcy was yet in evidence anywhere on the grounds. In truth, it was becoming increasingly more difficult to locate *anyone* in the Carella back yard. Immediately following the ceremony, the Carella household had been overrun by wedding guests who hugged and embraced and kissed each other as if they had not seen each other since the last wedding or funeral—which, in all probability, they hadn't. The bedroom and adjoining bathroom on the main floor of the Carella home had been set aside for the female guests, another similar setup upstairs having been made available for the gentlemen. As soon as all the embracing and kissing was concluded, the women trotted into the downstairs bedroom to freshen up, so that there was a constant flow of traffic from back yard to back porch to bedroom to bathroom and out again. Hawes was getting somewhat dizzy. In all that sea of strange faces, he longed only to see the vaguely familiar faces of Darcy and Jones, but for the time being he seemed to have lost them completely.

"What's the matter?" Christine asked him.

"I'm just wondering where Darcy and Jones went."

"Oh, they're probably around somewhere."

"Yes, but where?"

"Have you tried the men's room?"

"No."

"Why don't you?"

"All right, I will. Don't pick up any stray men while I'm gone."

"Now, Cotton, would *I* do a thing like that?"

"Yes."

He went into the house. A woman coming out of the bedroom said to another woman, "She's pregnant *again*, can you imagine? I haven't been to a wedding in the past five years that she hasn't been pregnant."

"She likes children," her friend said.

"*That* isn't what she likes," the woman said, and they both laughed hysterically, almost bumping into Hawes as he made his way to the steps.

"Oh, excuse *me*," the first woman said. Tittering, they went out of the house. Hawes climbed upstairs. The bedroom was cluttered with near and distant relatives of the Carellas and Giordanos. A tall, blue-eyed blond man lounging against the doorjamb said, "Full house, Mac."

"Mmm," Hawes said. "I'll wait."

"We got a choice?" the blond said.

"The Thunderbird ain't a sports car," a man near them said to his friend. "And neither is the Corvette. I got news for you, Charlie. There ain't no such animal as an American sports car."

"No?" Charlie said. "Then how come they call them sports cars?"

"What do you want they should call them: armored tanks? You know something?"

"What?" Charlie said.

"When a *real* sports-car owner passes an American sports car on the road, he don't even wave."

"So what?"

"So that's the sign of courtesy, like tipping your hat to a broad. And they don't do it. Because American sports cars ain't sports cars. They're considered like cockroaches on the road. That's a fact."

"Then what's a sports car?" Charlie asked.

"An MG, or a Jaguar, or a Talbot, or an Alfa Romeo, or a Ferrari, or Ghia, or . . ."

"All right, all right," Charlie said.

". . . or a Mercedes-Benz, or a . . ."

"All right," Charlie said, "I come up here to go to the john, not to hear a lecture about foreign cars."

The door to the bathroom opened. A slender man wearing eyeglasses stepped out, zipping his fly.

"Anybody else in there?" Hawes asked him.

"What?"

"In the bathroom."

"No," the bespectacled man said. "Of course not. Who else would be in there with me?" He paused. Indignantly, he said, "Who are you?"

"Water Commissioner," Hawes said. "Just checking."

"Oh." The man paused. "Everything okay?"

"Yes, fine, thank you." He took a last look around the bedroom. No. No Darcy or Jones. He was starting downstairs again when a cheer went up from the back yard. For a moment, Hawes thought the caterers had struck oil. And then he realized what it was.

"They're here!" someone shouted. "They're here!"

And at that instant, Sal Martino's orchestra began playing "Here Comes the Bride." Hawes joined the general exodus down the steps. Women were pouring out of the downstairs bedroom. Children were screaming and giggling, rushing onto the back porch, anxious for a glimpse of the newly arrived bride and groom. Sighing, Hawes vowed never to get married.

When he got out to the porch at last, he found Christine talking to Sam Jones.

"Well, well," he said, "this is a surprise. Where've you been, Jonesy?"

"Why? Someone looking for me?"

"No, I was just curious."

"Oh, I've been roaming around," Jonesy said.

Hawes looked at him curiously and skeptically. Sal Martino's boys were pounding out their third chorus of "Here Comes the Bride." The music trailed off lamely as the piano player attempted a modulation into another key. Failing, he blinked helplessly at Martino who gave the band a one-two-three count and, waving his trombone frantically, led them into "Let Me Call You Sweetheart."

The master of ceremonies, supplied by the caterers, rushed onto the floor, directing Tommy to dance with Angela. He needed no prompting.

"Best man!" the caterer shouted. "Maid of honor!"

"Excuse me," Jonesy said, and he rushed over to the long wooden rectangle which had been put down as a dance floor, ringed in by the long white tables. He took the maid of honor into his arms, and the MC beamed happily and then began pairing off ushers and bridesmaids, Tony and Louisa Carella, Steve and Teddy, and anyone else he saw in a tuxedo or a gown. The band *segued* into "Always," and the MC beamed some more, and then pulled Angela from Tommy's grasp and shoved her into Jonesy's arms, filling the void with the maid of honor whom Tommy accepted with a slightly dismayed smile. Ushers and bridesmaids began changing partners. Paunch to paunch, Tony Carella and his daughter-in-law whirled about the floor. Louisa Carella found herself in her son's arms.

"So?" Carella said. "Are you happy, Mom?"

"Yes. It was a beautiful wedding, Stevie. You should have got married in church."

"Now, stop it."

"All right, you big atheist."

"I'm not."

"You don't go to church."

"I work on Sundays."

"Only sometimes."

The band had somehow successfully modulated into "The Anniversary Waltz." The MC waved his arms at the people lining the dance floor, and they began filtering onto it, two by two, joining the wedding party. Tommy politely but firmly deposited the maid of honor into Jonesy's grip and pulled his bride to him. A tall red-headed girl in a green silk dress which had surely been applied with a spray gun, suddenly broke away from her partner and shouted, "Steve! Steve Carella!"

Carella turned. The redhead's voice was not exactly what he'd have called dulcet. It boomed across the dance floor with all the energy of a nuclear explosion. Teddy Carella, dancing with her father-in-law, happened to turn just as the redhead threw her arms around Carella's neck and planted a kiss on his mouth.

Carella blinked.

"Steve," the redhead said, "don't you remember me? Don't you remember Faye?"

Carella seemed to be having a little difficulty with the memory. He seemed also to be having a little difficulty with Faye herself whose arms were still firmly entwined about his neck. The green silk dress, in addition to having been sprayed on, was cut low in the front, very low. Glancing over the girl's shoulder, Carella saw Teddy whirl by in his father's arms, and he saw a frown beginning on her face.

"I . . . I . . ." he stammered, "don't seem to . . ."

"New Jersey?" the girl prompted. "Flemington? The wedding? Don't you remember? Oh, how we danced!"

Dimly, Carella remembered a wedding years and years ago. God, he must have been eighteen and yes, there was a redhead, a slender, bosomy girl of seventeen, and yes, he'd danced with her all night, and yes, her name was Faye, and oh my God!

"Hello, Faye," he said weakly.

"Come!" Faye commanded. "Dance with me! You don't mind, do you, Mrs. Carella?"

"No," Louisa said, "but . . ." and she shot an apprehensive glance across the floor to Teddy, who was craning her neck over her shoulder to observe any new developments.

Faye pulled Carella to her. She threw her left arm up around his neck and Carella was overpowered by the scent of a heady perfume which drifted into his nostrils. Faye put her cheek against his.

"How have you been, Steve?" she asked.

And Carella answered, "Married."

Across the floor, Ben Darcy cut in on Tommy Giordano. Tommy, surprised, did not relinquish his bride for a moment.

"Come on," Ben said, smiling. "You've got to share the wealth."

Graciously, Tommy bowed and handed Angela to Ben. They danced in silence for several moments.

Then Ben said, "Happy?"

"Yes."

"Do you love him?"

"Oh, yes," Angela said. "Yes, yes!"

"I used to hope . . . well, you know."

"What, Ben?"

"We saw an awful lot of each other when we were kids, Angela."

"Yes, I know."

"You told me you loved me."

"I know I did. We were kids, Ben."

"I loved you, Angela."

"Ben . . ."

"I've never met another girl like you, do you know that?"

"I think they'll be serving soon. Maybe we'd better . . ."

"Never a girl as pretty as you, or as smart as you, or as warm and exciting as . . ."

"Ben, please!"

"I'm sorry, Angela. It's just . . . I used to think this would be us. It could have been us, you know."

"Everyone grows up, Ben."

"Angela, you once said . . . when we were younger . . . when you first met Tommy . . . I called you, I remember, and you told me it was all over between us. Do you remember that?"

"Yes, Ben. I do."

"You shouldn't have ended it on the telephone. Not after what we'd been to each other."

"I'm sorry. I suppose . . . I just wanted it to be clean, Ben. Over with. Done. I didn't want one of those long, drawn-out . . ."

"I know, I know. And okay, I don't mind. But . . . when I was talking to you on the phone, I said if . . . if anything ever went wrong between you and Tommy, I'd be waiting. Remember that?"

"Yes. I remember."

"And you said, 'All right, Ben. I'll keep that in mind.' Do you remember saying that?"

"It was such a long time ago, Ben. I really don't . . ."

"I'm still waiting, Angela."

"What?"

"If anything should go wrong, if anything at all should happen between you, I'll be here. You can count on me. I'll take you in a minute, Angela. I loved you once, Angela, and I still . . ."

"Ben, please stop it. Please."

"Just remember. I'll be waiting for you. I'll be waiting, Angela."

The Green Corner was a tree-shaded house with a winding walk lined with azalea bushes in full bloom. Meyer and O'Brien walked leisurely to the front door and rang the bell.

"Coming," a voice said, and they waited as footsteps approached the door. The door opened. A wispy little woman in a dark-blue dress stood there, smiling. From somewhere in the house, a dog began barking.

"Hello," she said.

"Hello," Meyer answered. "Are you the lady of the house?"

"My, do they send salesmen around on Sundays, too?" the little woman asked.

"No, we're from the police," Meyer said. The smile dropped from the little woman's mouth. "Now, don't be alarmed," he added hastily. "We only wanted to—"

"I'm only the dog sitter," the little woman said. "I dont even live here. I don't know anything about any lawbreaking that's been going on. I come to sit with the dog, that's all."

"No one's broken any law," O'Brien said, "We only wanted to ask some questions, lady."

"Well, I don't know anything about anyone who lives here. I only sit with the dog. His name is Butch, and he tears up the furniture if they leave him alone, he gets so lonely and miserable. So I sit with him. Butch is the only one I know here."

"Do you know the owners of the house?"

"Mr. and Mrs. Travers, yes, but not so good as I know Butch. Butch is a Golden Retriever, but he chews up the furniture. Which is why . . ."

"Know any of the roomers?"

"Yes, there's old Mr. Van Ness on the top floor, but he's out right now. And there's Mrs. Wittley, but she's out, too. And then there's the new girl, Oona Blake, but she's out, too. And I don't know any of them real good except Butch. He's the only reason I come over here. I'm one of the best dog sitters in the neighborhood."

"This Oona Blake," O'Brien said. "Is it Miss or Mrs.?"

"Miss, of course. Why, she's just a young girl."

"How old?"

"Not thirty yet, I would say."

"You said she's out right now. Do you know what time she left?"

"Yes. Early this morning. I know because the Traverses are away for the weekend which is why I'm sitting with Butch. I got here yesterday. And I was here this morning when Miss Blake left."

"What time would you say that was?"

"Right after breakfast. I also make the meals when the Traverses are gone."

"Did anyone call for her?"

"Who? Mrs. Travers?"

"No. Miss Blake."

"Oh. Oh, yes. As a matter of fact, someone did."

"Who?"

"Don't know him. I told you, I don't know much of the goings-on here. You ask me, the Traverses run this place too loose. Too loose."

"Was the man carrying anything?"

"What man?"

"The man who picked up Miss Blake."

"Oh. Him. Yes, he was. A trombone case."

"A trombone case? Not a trumpet? Or a saxophone?"

"No, a trombone. Don't I know a trombone when I see one? A long black case. Oh, it was a trombone, all right."

"What did he look like?"

"I didn't get a good look. He was sitting in the parlor waiting for her, and the shades were drawn. But I saw the trombone case leaning against the armchair." The little woman paused. "She won't be here long, anyway. That Oona Blake."

"What makes you say that?"

"I was dog-sitting last week. She got three calls in the same day. All from the same place. A real estate agent. She'll be moving soon, that one."

"Which real estate agent? Do you recall the name?"

"Certainly. She got three calls in the same day. Besides, it isn't far from here."

"What's the name?" O'Brien asked.

"Pullen Real Estate. It's the next elevated stop from here. Right on the corner, under the station."

"Can you tell us what Oona Blake looks like?" Meyer asked.

"Yes, certainly. But I don't really know very much about her. Where shall I start?"

"What was she wearing when she left here this morning?"

"A red silk dress, rather low cut. Red high-heeled pumps. No stockings. A little sort of red feather in her hair, with a rhinestone clip."

"Was she carrying a purse?"

"One of these small things that all you can fit into are a compact and lipstick and a few odds and ends."

"Was that red, too?"

"No. It was a dark blue. Sequins, I believe."

"And how would you describe *her?*"

"She's a blonde. I think it's natural. She's very well developed. If you ask me, she's got a thyroid condition. Anyway, she's a very big girl. Noisy, I guess. Or perhaps she just talks loud. She's very pretty, I would say. Blue eyes. She gives an impression of . . . I don't know . . . being strong, I guess. She's got a nice smile and a pretty nose. Does that help?"

"Yes. Thank you very much."

"You going to that real estate office now?"

"Yes."

"I wouldn't. He's closed on Sundays."

The girl dancing with Bert Kling was wearing a red silk dress and red high-heeled pumps. She wore a red feather in her hair, and the feather tickled Kling's cheek as he maneuvered her over the makeshift dance floor. People were beginning to filter to the tables where cocktails had been placed at each setting. Kling was beginning to feel a little hungry. Perhaps it was the way the girl danced, with a sort of nervous, pushing energy that demanded all his leading skill to counter. She was a very busty girl, and she danced quite close, her long blond hair brushing his cheek. She seemed quite feminine and lovely—even though she was a big girl—but there was

nonetheless this pushing quality about her which gave
him the feeling that *she* was leading *him* around the dance
floor. The strength seemed in direct contradiction to the
blue eyes and lovely smile which had first attracted him
to her. The eyes and the smile had been totally female.
The dancing was the footwork of a steel magnate, a person with something to do, a person anxious to get it done.

The band, once one got used to it, wasn't really half
bad. Playing a medley of foxtrots, they moved smoothly
from one number to the next, keeping a steady danceable
beat. Sal Martino had put his trombone on a chair which
rested on the bandstand alongside him, and he led the
orchestra with his right hand, smiling out at the crowd
occasionally. Waiters rushed across the lawn carrying
drinks. Kling's eyes moved across the dance floor. Ben
Darcy was still dancing with Angela. The pair seemed
to be having an argument. Steve Carella was dancing with
a redhead who'd undoubtedly leaped from the pages of
Playboy although, Kling mused, the same observation
could probably be made about the blonde who was pushing him around the floor. Teddy Carella didn't look too
damn happy about the inflammable girl in the green dress.
Cotton Hawes didn't look too happy, either. Dismally, he
watched Christine Maxwell dancing with Sam Jones.

This is one hell of a wedding, Kling thought. Everybody bursting with joy. Even Steve looks pretty gloomy,
though I can't see why that readhead should make any
man gloomy.

"I don't think I know your name," Kling said to the
blonde in the red dress.

"You don't" she answered. Her voice was deep and
husky.

"Mine's Bert."

"Nice to know you," the blonde said.

He waited for her to offer her name. When she didn't,
he let it pass. What the hell, if a girl didn't want to give
her name, there was no sense forcing her. Besides, he

told himself in deference to his fiancée, he was only dancing so that he wouldn't look conspicuous standing on the sidelines.

"You a relative?" he asked.

"No." The girl paused. "Are you?"

"No." Kling paused. "Friend of the bride?"

The girl hesitated for just a fraction of a second. Then she said, "Yes."

"Nice wedding," Kling said.

"Lovely," the girl agreed, and she continued to push him around the floor as if in a hurry to get nowhere particularly fast.

On the bandstand, Sal Martino leaned over to pick up his trombone.

From the corner of his eye, Kling caught the movement. He turned to face the bandleader. Sal's coat fell open as he picked up the horn. He stood up quickly then, the horn in both hands.

Kling's arm tightened involuntarily around the blonde's waist.

"Hey," she said. "Easy does it, boy."

Kling released her. "Excuse me, miss," he said, and he left her standing in the middle of the dance floor.

Teddy Carella sat at the table alongside the bride's table, sipping disconsolately at a Manhattan, watching her husband cavort in the arms of a redheaded sexpot from Flemington, New Jersey.

This is not fair, she thought angrily. There is no competition here. I don't know who that damn girl is, or what she wants—although what she wants seems pretty apparent—but I do know that she is svelte and trim and wearing a dress designed for a size 8. Since she is at least a 10, and possibly a 12, the odds are stacked against me to begin with. I am at least a size 54 right now. When will this baby come? Next week did the doctor say? Yes, next week. Next week and four thousand years from now. I've

been big forever. I hope it's a boy. Mark, if it's a boy.
Mark Carella. That's a good name.

Steve, you don't have to hold her so damn close!
I mean, *really*, goddamnit!

And April if it's a girl.

I wonder if I should faint or something. That would
bring him back to the table in a hurry, all right. Although
I can't really say that *he's* holding her close because *she*
seems to be doing all the holding. But I guess holding
works both ways, and don't think this has been easy on
me, Steve, my pet, and you really needn't . . . Steve! If
your hand moves another inch, I am going to crown you
with a champagne bottle!

She watched as Bert Kling pushed his way through the
dancers, heading for her husband.

Is he going to cut in? she wondered.

And then Kling's hand clamped down on Carella's
shoulder, and he backed away from the redhead as Kling
whispered something in his ear.

Carella blinked.

"What? What did you say?"

In a hurried whisper, Kling repeated, "The bandleader! He's carrying a gun under his coat!"

Chapter 8

SAL MARTINO didn't look very happy at all.

The detectives had waited until the intermission and
then, as the waiters began serving the shrimp cocktail,
they'd approached the bandstand, asked him to accompany them, and led him upstairs to a small bedroom in
the Carella house. They stood before him in a three-man
semicircle, now, Hawes, Carella, and Kling. Their faces
were humorless and grim.

"Why are you carrying a gun?" Carella said.

"Who wants to know?" Sal answered.

"I do. I'm a detective. Do you want to see my badge?"

"Yes. I do. What is this, anyway?"

Carella flipped open his wallet. "It's a few questions, Sal," he said. "We want to know about that gun under your jacket. Now what the hell are you doing with a gun?"

Sal studied the shield. "That's my business," he said. "You got no right to ask me. What the hell is this? A police state?"

"Give me the gun," Carella said.

"What for?"

"Give it to me!" he snapped.

Sal dug into the shoulder holster under his jacket.

"Butt first," Carella said.

Sal handed him the gun. Carella looked at it, and then gave it to Hawes. "An Iver Johnson .22," he said.

"Protector Sealed Eight," Hawes agreed, and he sniffed the barrel.

"What the hell are you smelling?" Sal wanted to know. "That hasn't been fired in years."

"Why are you carrying it?" Carella asked.

"That's my business."

"It's my business, too," Carella shouted. "Now don't get snotty with me, Martino. Answer the questions!"

"I told you. Why I carry a gun is my business and my business alone. And you can go straight to hell!"

"Did you ever try playing the trombone with a busted arm?" Hawes asked quietly.

"What?"

"*Why are you carrying a gun?*" Hawes shouted.

"I got a permit."

"Let's see it."

"I don't have to show you nothing."

"If you've got a permit, show it," Kling said. "Because if you don't, I'm going straight to that telephone and call the local precinct, and you can explain it all to them in the squadroom. Now how about it, Martino?"

"I told you I got a permit."

"Then let's see it!"

"a permit and can't show it, you lose it. That's the law. Now let's see it."

"You invent your own laws, don't you?" Martino said, digging into his wallet.

"Is it carry or premises?"

"It's carry. You think I'd be lugging a gun around with a premises permit?"

"Where is it?"

"Just a minute, just a minute," Martino said. He pulled a document out of his wallet and then unfolded it. He handed it to Carella. "There," he said. "You satisfied now?"

2378*

CITY BUREAU OF PISTOL PERMITS

DATE June 9 1958 LICENSE TO __Carry__ PISTOL IS HEREBY GRANTED

TO __Salvatore Albert Martino__

STREET ADDRESS __583 Avalon Avenue__

CITY OR TOWN __Riverhead__

OCCUPATION __Musician__

EMPLOYED BY __Self-employed__

NATIONALITY __U.S.A.__

AGE __28__ HEIGHT __5'9"__ WEIGHT __157__

Arthur K. Weidman
MUNICIPAL MAGISTRATE, RIVERHEAD

The document was divided into three sections separated by perforated folding edges. It was printed on a dull shade of off-pink paper. Its outer edges were serrated. Each section measured 4½ inches by 3¾ inches.

Carella took the small official-looking document from Martino and studied the first section.

Carella read each item carefully. Then he turned the permit over to read its reverse side:

This license is issued under the following conditions:
1. It is good until revoked.
2. It is revocable at any time.
3. It is VOID for any defacement or change on permit. Holder of VOID permit subject to Penal Law, Section 1897.
4. It is restricted to ~~target shooting~~, present employment, or _____
5. To add additional guns, apply for amended permit.

Salvatore A. Martino
SIGNATURE OF HOLDER

Make	Caliber	Number
Iver Johnson	.22	326912

Thumb Print

"All right, all right, hold your water. I don't have to show it to you, you know. I'm doing you a favor."

"You're doing yourself a favor, Martino. If you've got

The third section of the permit simply granted Martino permission to purchase a pistol and was signed by the same Riverhead magistrate, Arthur K. Weidman.

Carella knew at once that the permit was legitimate. He nonetheless took his sweet time examining it. He turned it over in his big hands as if it were a questionable international document prepared by Russian spies. He studied the signature, and he studied the thumb print, and he made a great show of comparing the serial number on the permit with the number stamped into the metal of Martino's .22.

Then he handed both gun and permit back to the trombonist.

"Now suppose you tell us why you carry it, Sal?"

"I don't have to. The permit is enough. I got a gun, and I got a permit for it, and that's all you have to know. If you don't mind, I'm supposed to play some dinner music."

"The dinner music can wait. Answer the question, Sal!" Kling said.

"I don't have to."

"We'd better pull him in," Hawes said.

"Pull me in? What for?" Martino yelled.

"For refusing to co-operate with a duly appointed officer of the peace," Hawes yelled right off the top of his head.

"Okay, okay, okay," Martino said in rising crescendo. "Okay."

"Well?"

"I'm scared."

"What?"

"I'm scared. I play on jobs, and sometimes I don't get home till three, four in the morning. I'm scared. I don't like to walk the streets so late at night carrying money and my horn. I'm scared, okay? So I applied for a pistol permit, and I got it. Because I'm scared, okay? Okay? Does that answer your goddamn question?"

"It answers us," Carella said, and he looked somewhat shamefacedly at his colleagues. "You'd better get back to the band."

Martino folded his pistol permit in half and then shoved it back into his wallet, alongside his driver's license.

"There's no law against being afraid," he said.

"If there were," Carella answered, "we'd all be in jail."

"Here it is," Meyer Meyer called to the counter. "Donald Pullen, 131 Pondigo Street . . . no, wait, that's the office. It's 4251 Archer. That's around here, isn't it?"

"Search me," O'Brien said. "We'd better ask a cop. You looked up the number too fast, Meyer. I haven't finished my coffee yet."

"Well, hurry up."

Patiently, Meyer waited for O'Brien to gulp down his coffee.

"I've been thirsting for this cup of coffee all day," O'Brien said. "I've got to work out that problem with Miscolo. Do you think maybe I can subtly hint that he change brands or something?"

"I don't think that'd work, Bob."

"No, I don't think so, either."

"Why don't you bring your own coffeepot to the office? And buy yourself a hot plate? One of those single-burner jobs."

"Gee, that sounds like a good idea," O'Brien said. "Except for one thing."

"What's that?"

"I don't know how to make coffee."

"All right, come on, drink up."

O'Brien finished his coffee. Together, they walked out to the unmarked police sedan parked at the curb.

"4251 Archer," Meyer said. "We'll ask the first traffic cop we see."

They did not see a cop for ten blocks. They pulled over to him and asked him where Archer Street was.

"Archer Avenue, you mean?"

"Yes, I guess so."

"So say what the hell you mean. And pull over to the curb. You're blocking traffic!"

"We only want to know . . ."

"I know what you want to know. You giving me an argument?"

"No, sir," Meyer said, and he pulled to the curb and

waited while the cop directed the cars behind him. Finally, the cop walked over to the car.

"Don't you know better than to stop in the middle of the street?" he asked.

"I wasn't thinking, Officer," Meyer said.

"Sure. Now what was it you wanted to know?"

"How to get to Archer Avenue."

"Two blocks down and turn right. What number did you want?"

"4251," Meyer said.

"Another three blocks after you make the turn." He glanced at the oncoming traffic. "Okay, go ahead." As they pulled away, he shouted, *"And don't stop in the middle of the street no more, you hear me, mister?"*

"Nice fellow," Meyer said.

"Gives cops a bad name," O'Brien said glumly.

"Why? He helped us, didn't he?"

"Bad disposition," O'Brien said, and Meyer made his right turn. "Three blocks from here, right?"

"Right," Meyer said. They drove up the street leisurely and stopped before 4251. "Here it is. Let's hope he's home."

4251 Archer, as were most of the dwellings in Riverhead, was a private house. Meyer and O'Brien went up the front walk and pulled the door knocker. A tall man in a white shirt and a red weskit answered the door.

"Yes, gentlemen," he said, "can I help you?"

"Mr. Pullen?" Meyer said.

"Yes?" Pullen studied his visitors. "Is it real estate, or insurance?"

"We'd like to ask you some questions, Mr. Pullen. We're from the police."

"Police?" Pullen went white in the space of two seconds. "Wh— wh— what . . . what did . . . ?"

"May we come in, Mr. Pullen?"

"Yes. Yes, come in." Hastily, Pullen glanced past

them to make sure none of his neighbors were watching. "Come in."

They followed him into the house and into the living room. The room was done in heavy furniture covered with maroon mohair. It made the small interior seem hotter than it really was.

"Sit down," Pullen said. "What's this all about?"

"Have you been receiving or making phone calls to a Miss Oona Blake?"

"Why, yes." Pullen looked surprised, and then relieved. "Oh, it's about *her*, isn't it? Not me? Her?"

"Yes, it's about her."

"I knew she was a tough customer. I knew it the minute I laid eyes on her. A very flashy person. Very flashy. What is she? A prostitute?"

"No, we don't know what she is. We'd simply like to find out what the nature of her business with you was."

"Why, real estate," Pullen said. "What did you think? She wanted to rent an apartment."

"Where?"

"Well, she was very specific about it. She wanted an apartment either facing 831 Charles Avenue or else *behind* 831 Charles Avenue. That's just a little ways from here. Charles Avenue."

"That rings a bell," Meyer said. He thought for a moment. "Sure. That's where Steve's parents live. Did Miss Blake say why she wanted an apartment near that address?"

"Said she had friends there."

"I see. Did you get an apartment for her?"

"Nope. Not that one. But I was able to *fill* her other request. Yep, I gave her good service on that one."

"Which one was that?" O'Brien asked.

Pullen smiled. "Why, the apartment she wanted near the photography studio."

"What a dinner!" Birnbaum said. "Tony, you outdid yourself. What a wedding, what a dinner!"

"Birnbaum, have some champagne," Tony said. "We got enough champagne here to start a France. Have some champagne, my friend." He led Birnbaum to the ice mermaid and pulled a bottle from her frozen tub. Everywhere around him, champagne corks were popping, and each new pop filled Tony's heart with joy. It really was getting to be a fine wedding. Maybe all the money those lousy Incorporates were getting would be worth it after all. He tore the gold foil from the neck of the bottle and then ripped the wire loose. Working the cork with his thumbs, he slowly edged it out of the bottle. Standing next to him, Birnbaum put his fingers in his ears. The cork moved out of the bottle neck.

"POP!" Tony shouted, and the cork exploded from the bottle at the same instant, white bubbles following it out of the green neck, spilling onto Tony's thick fingers. Birnbaum clapped Tony on the back, and they began laughing uproariously. The band was playing louder, and Jody Lewis was running all over the lawn popping his flash bulbs, capturing the bride and groom for posterity. He followed them to the long bridal table where the ancient and time-honored custom of collecting the connubial loot was about to take place. Angela made a beautiful hostess for the receiving line. Tommy sat beside her, grinning from ear to ear, and Jody Lewis kept the shutter clicking as the relatives filed past to kiss the bride and wish her luck, to shake hands with the groom and congratulate him. During the shaking of hands, a gratuity, a present, a ten-dollar bill or a twenty-dollar bill in an envelope was pressed into Tommy's hand.

"Congratulations," the well-wishers said, slightly embarrassed by the handing over of money, a civilized gesture with all the inherent savagery of primitive times, the spoils offered to the newly crowned king. And Tommy, in turn, was embarrassed as he accepted the gifts because there is nothing more difficult to do than accept a gift with style, and Tommy was too young to have acquired style. "Thank you," he muttered over and over again. "Thank you, thank you."

The champagne corks kept exploding.

"The trouble with this stuff," Birnbaum says, "is it makes you want to go to the bathroom."

"So go," Tony said.

"I will."

"Right upstairs. The bedroom at the end of the . . ."

"No, no. Too crowded up there," Birnbaum said. "I'll run over to my own house."

"What? And miss the wedding?"

"It'll take a minute. It'll be quick. Don't worry, Tony, I'll be back. Just try to keep me away."

"All right, Birnbaum. Hurry! Hurry!"

Birnbaum cocked his head to one side and started off through the bushes to his house on the next lot.

At the far end of the table, unobserved by either Angela or Tommy who were busy accepting gifts and good wishes, a pair of hands deposited a pair of small bottles filled with red wine. The bottles of wine were each tied with big bows. One bow was pink, the other was blue.

The pink bow had attached to it a card which read:

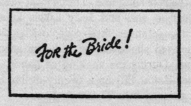

The blue bow had attached to it a similar card which, had Tommy seen it, might have struck a responsive chord. It is doubtful, however, that he would have recognized the handwriting as being identical with that on a card he'd received earlier in the day.

The card attached to the blue bow read, simply:

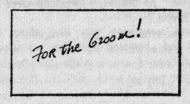

For the Groom!

"Come with me," Jonesy said to Christine.

"I came here with someone, you know," Christine said coyly. She was rather enjoying the game and, oddly because she had not wanted to come, she was enjoying the wedding, too. But particularly, she was enjoying the look of dismay which spread over Cotton's face whenever he saw her dancing with Sam Jones. The look was priceless. She enjoyed it more than the music, and more than the champagne, and more than the exploding corks, and the wonderful free feeling of gaiety which pervaded the outdoor reception.

"I know you came with someone. He's bigger than me, too," Jonesy said, "but I don't care. Come on."

"Where are you taking me?" Christine said, giggling as Jonesy pulled her by the hand into the bushes at the side of the house. "Jonesy! Really now!"

"Come, come, come," he said. "I want to show you something." He dragged her deeper into the bushes onto a path which had been stamped down through constant walking through the short grass.

"What do you want to show me?"

"Let's get a little further away from the festivities first," he said. His hand on hers was tight. He pulled her along the path as if urgently propelled. Christine was not frightened. She was, in truth, slightly excited. She thought she knew what was coming, and she thought she would not resist what was coming. It would serve Cotton right if a handsome young stranger dragged her into the bushes like a caveman and kissed her soundly and completely.

No, she would not resist.

There was something very nice about the attention Sam Jones had showered upon her all afternoon, something reminiscent of a time when she'd been very young, when outdoor parties were standard fare every weekend during the summer. Now, running over the short grass with him, she looked forward to the kiss she knew was coming. She felt very youthful all at once, a young girl running through a tree-shaded lane, her feet dancing over the sunlight-speckled trampled path at the far end of the lot.

Jonesy stopped suddenly.

"Here," he said. "This should be far enough away, don't you think?"

"For what?" Christine asked. Oddly, her heart was pounding in her chest.

"Don't you know?" Jonesy said. He pulled her toward him, his back to the Carella property. Christine felt suddenly breathless. She lifted her mouth for his kiss, and someone suddenly screamed, and she felt goose pimples erupt over every inch of her body, and then she realized it was Jonesy who was screaming, screaming in a wildly masculine voice, and she pulled away from him and looked into his face and then turned to follow his glazed stare.

Not seven feet from where they were standing, a man lay face downward on the path. The man's back was covered with blood. The man was not breathing.

"Oh my God!" Jonesy said. "It's Birnbaum!"

Chapter 9

THE TELEPHONE in the squadroom was ringing insistently.

Hal Willis, alone, unbent from his doubled-over position alongside the water cooler and shouted, "All right, all right, for Christ's sake! It never fails. A guy goes for a drink of water and . . . all right, I'm coming!" He threw water and paper cup into the trash basket and ran like hell for the phone, snatching it from the receiver.

"Hello!" he shouted. "Eighty-seventh Squad!" he shouted. "Detective Willis speaking!" he shouted.

"I can hear you, Mac," the voice said. "I can almost hear you without the aid of the instrument, and I'm all the way down on High Street. Shall we try it again? *Pizzicato* this time?"

"You mean *diminuendo,* don't you?" Willis said softly.

"Whatever I mean, I think we all get the idea. This is Avery Atkins at the lab. Somebody up there sent a note down to us. We've been working on it."

"What note?"

"It says 'For the groom.' Familiar with it?"

"Vaguely. What about it?"

"What did you say your name was, friend?"

"Willis. Hal Willis. Detective 3rd/Grade. Male, white, American."

"*And* pretty snotty," Atkins said.

"Listen, have you got information for me, or have you? I'm all alone here, and I've got a million things to do. So how about it?"

"Here it is. Catch it, wise guy. Paper used was five-and-dime stuff, trade name Skyline, sold over the counter all over the city at twenty-five cents for a package of ten cards and ten little envelopes. Go chase that one down. Ink used was Sheaffer's Skrip, number 32, permanent jet black. Ditto over counters across the face of our fair city. You can chase that one down, too, wise guy. Which brings us to fingerprints. Two sets on the card, both lousy. One set belongs to a guy named Thomas Giordano. No record. Checked it through his service fingerprints, he was in the Army Signal Corps. The second set belongs to a guy named Stephen Louis Carella who, I understand, is a detective working for the magnificent 87th Squad. He ought to be careful where he lays his fat fingers. You had enough, smart guy?"

"I'm still listening."

"Comes to the handwriting itself, and there's a lot of crap here you don't have to know about unless you come up with a sample for comparison. There's only one thing you do have to know."

"What's that?"

"Whoever sent this over asked us to run a handwriting comparison against the signature of one Martin Sokolin on whom we have a record at the IB. We did that. And one thing's for sure."

"And what's that?"

"Martin Sokolin didn't write that love note."

The three detectives stood over the body of Joseph Birnbaum. There was no pain, no joy, no sorrow on their faces. Impassively, they stared at death and whatever they felt was rigidly concealed behind the masks they wore for society.

Carella was the first to kneel.

"Shot him in the back," he said. "Bullet probably passed through to the heart. Killed him instantly."

"That's my guess," Hawes said, nodding.

"How come we didn't hear the shot?" Kling asked.

"All those champagne bottles going off. This is quite a distance from the house. The shot probably sounded like just another cork going off. Take a look around, will you, Bert? See if you can find the spent cartridge."

Kling began thrashing through the bushes. Carella turned to Jonesy where he stood with Christine. His face was a pasty white. His hands, though he tried to control them, were trembling at his sides.

"Pull yourself together," Carella said harshly. "You can help us, but not the way you are now."

"I . . . I . . . I can't help it," Jonesy said. "I . . . I feel like I'm going to collapse. That's why . . . why I sent Christine for you."

"Is that why?" Hawes asked.

"I . . . I knew I couldn't make it myself."

"Maybe it's a good thing," Carella said. "If you'd have erupted onto that lawn, you'd have busted up that wedding as sure as . . ."

"What were you doing back here, anyway?" Hawes said, and he looked at Christine angrily.

"We were taking a walk," Jonesy said.

"Why here?"

"Why not?"

"Answer my question, damnit!" Hawes shouted. "That man there is dead, and you're the one who found the body, and I'd like to know just what the hell brought you back here? Coincidence?"

"Yes."

"Why? What were you doing here?"

"Walking with Christine."

"Cotton, we just . . ."

"I'll get to you, Christine," Hawes said. "Why'd you choose this path for a walk, Jones? So that you'd have a witness when you discovered the body?"

"What?"

"You heard me!"

"That's . . . that's prep—that's preposterous!"

"Is it? Then why'd you come back here?"

"So I could kiss Christine," Jonesy blurted.

"And did you?" Hawes said venomously.

"Cotton . . ."

"Keep out of this, Christine. Did you kiss her?"

"What's this got to do with Birnbaum? What business is it of yours whether or not I . . ."

"When did you see the body?" Carella interrupted, annoyed because Hawes was dragging his interrogation down into the muck of a private and not a police matter.

"We were standing here," Jonesy said. "And I happened to see it."

"You were just standing here?" Carella asked.

"I . . . I was going to kiss Christine."

"Go on," Carella said, and he watched Hawes's fists close into hard balls at his sides.

"I saw the body," Jonesy said. "And I—I screamed. And then I recognized it was Birnbaum."

"Where does this path lead?" Hawes snapped.

"To Birnbaum's house. On the next lot."

Kling came thrashing through the bushes. "Here it is, Steve," he said, and he held out the brass casing. Carella looked at it. The side of the casing was stamped "357 MAGNUM." The back end of the casing had the lettering fixed in a circle:

In any case, there was no doubt about what kind of a gun had fired this particular cartridge. Either a Colt or a Smith & Wesson Magnum revolver.

"A Magnum," Carella said. "A big gun."

"Not necessarily," Hawes said. "Smith & Wesson puts out a Magnum with a short three-and-a-half-inch barrel."

"In any event, this casing lets out our friend Martino with his Iver Johnson .22."

"Yeah. What do we do now, Steve?"

"Call Homicide, I guess. With three detectives on the scene, I don't think we ought to ring the local squad. Or should we?"

"I think we'd better."

"Jesus, I'd hate like hell to break up the wedding." He paused. "I don't think Birnbaum would have wanted that, either."

"Maybe we won't have to."

"How do you figure?"

"This spot is pretty well protected from your father's lot. Maybe we can bring the photographers and the ME in through the next street, across Birnbaum's back yard and through the bushes. What do you think?"

"I don't know," Carella said.

"What precinct is this, anyway?"

"The 112th, I think."

"Know anybody on the squad?"

"No. Do you?"

"No."

"So what makes you think they'll do us a favor?"

"Professional courtesy. What the hell, it won't hurt asking. You only get married once."

Carella nodded and looked down at the lifeless body of Joseph Birnbaum, the neighbor. "You only die once, too," he said. "Come on, Jonesy, back to the house. You, too, Miss Maxwell. Few questions I'd like to ask both of you. Bert, you come back and call the 112th. Cotton, will you stay with the body?" He suspected that Hawes might be better equipped for the diplomacy necessary with the 112th Squad than Kling was. But at the same time, he didn't want a jealous male bellowing at an obviously frightened suspect while he questioned Jonesy and Christine further.

If Hawes appreciated Carella's tactic, he showed no sign of it. He simply nodded and went to stand alongside the prostrate Birnbaum as the rest started back for the house.

In the distance, Hawes could hear the sound of the band, the sound of voices raised in laughter, the tiny far-away pops of the champagne corks. Closer, the insects filled the woods with their myriad noises. He swatted at a fly which had settled on his nose, and then lighted a cigarette. The path, he noticed, took a sharp turn several feet beyond where Birnbaum was lying. Idly, Hawes walked to the bend in the path, surprised when the woods around him suddenly ended to become the open lawn of the Birnbaum back yard. He glanced up at the Birnbaum house.

Something glinted in the attic window.

He looked again.

There was a sudden movement, and then the window presented nothing more than a blank open rectangle.

But Hawes was certain he'd seen a man with a rifle in that window a second ago.

A blonde in a red silk dress was sitting at the dressing table in the downstairs bedroom when Christine Maxwell entered the room. Carella had told her he wanted to question Jonesy alone and that he would get back to her shortly. She'd gone downstairs immediately in search of the ladies' room. She wasn't feeling at all well, and she wanted to wash her face and put on some fresh lipstick.

If anything, the blonde in the red silk dress made her feel worse.

As Christine put her small blue purse down on the dressing table, the blonde was adjusting her stocking, the red dress pulled back over her nylon, her magnificently turned leg rivaling that in any Hollywood boudoir scene. Standing beside the blonde in the tight, low-cut, over-flowing-in-abundance red silk, standing beside the splendidly outstretched leg, Christine Maxwell felt suddenly skinny and awkward. She knew this was absurd. She'd always thought of herself as rather well-proportioned, capable of provoking a whistle or two on any street corner in the city. But the blonde who smoothed the nylon over her extended leg was so munificently endowed, so regally statuesque, that Christine suddenly imagined she'd been fooling herself all these years. The blonde tightened her garter, her shoulders and breasts bobbing with the movement. Fascinated, Christine watched the rippling flesh.

"You look kind of pale, honey," the blonde said.

"What? Oh, yes. I guess I do."

"Go out and have some of that whisky. Put the color back into your cheeks." She rose suddenly, looked at herself in the mirror, tucked a stray strand of hair back into place, and then said. "There, it's all yours. I've got to see John." She walked into the bathroom, closing and locking the door behind her.

Christine opened her purse, took out a comb, and began combing her hair. She did look pale. She'd better wash her face. God, that poor man lying in the path.

The bathroom door opened. "Well, so long, dear," the blonde said. She walked to the dressing table, snatched a purse from its top, and breezed out of the bedroom.

Apparently, she had not noticed that the purse she'd taken was Christine's.

Nor did Christine, in her agitated state, notice the error either.

Peering over the window sill, the man in the attic room of Birnbaum's empty house saw Hawes glance up at the window and then glance up at it again. Quickly, he ducked below the sill.

He saw me, he thought.

He saw the rifle.

Now what?

Goddamnit, she knows *she's supposed to keep anyone away from this house! Where the hell is she? Why isn't she doing what she's supposed to be doing?*

He waited, listening.

He could hear the steady crunch of heavy feet across the lawn behind the house. Cautiously, he crawled on his hands and knees to the left of the window, and then stood up. He backed away from the window. From where he stood, he could not be seen from outside, but he had a clear view of the lawn and . . . yes, that man was heading for the house, walking across the lawn at a brisk clip.

What do I do? he wondered.

He listened.

The man was coming around the side of the house. He heard footsteps on the slate walk there, and then on the steps leading to the front porch, and then clomping across the porch to stop at the front door. There was no knock. Stealthily, the front door eased open, creaking on its hinges.

Silence.

In the attic room, the sniper waited. He could hear the footsteps again, carefully, quietly advancing through the silent house, toward the steps, hesitating on each tread, each creaking step bringing the intruder closer and closer to the attic room. Quickly, the sniper went to the door and stood just inside it. Quickly, he grasped the rifle by its barrel.

There were cautious footsteps in the corridor outside now.

He held his breath and waited.

The doorknob twisted almost imperceptibly.

The sniper swung the rifle back over his shoulder like a ball bat.

Gun in hand, Cotton Hawes kicked open the door to the attic, and the rifle moved in a sudden blurring arc, the butt catching him on the side of his face and knocking him senseless to the floor.

Chapter 10

THE STENCH OF CORDITE still hung in the air of the small room across the street from Jody Lewis' photography shop. Donald Pullen opened the door with his key and then said, "Phew! What's that stink?"

"Cordite," Meyer said immediately. The smell was as familiar to him as the scent of his wife, though not nearly so pleasant. "Someone fired a gun in here, Bob."

"Yeah," O'Brien said, and immediately began looking for the spent shell casing.

Meyer went to the window. "Nice view of the photography shop," he said. He bent suddenly. "Here it is, Bob." He picked up the shell casing.

"Here's another one," O'Brien said. He carried the casing to Meyer.

"Same gun," Meyer said. "A rifle."

"Somebody fired a rifle in this room?" Pullen asked incredulously.

"It looks that way," Meyer said.

"Why? Why would anybody fire a rifle in a small room like this?"

"A good guess might be in order to hit somebody going in or coming out of that photography shop across the street. You said Miss Blake specifically requested an apartment near the photography shop, didn't you?"

"Why, yes! That's amazing," Pullen said. "That certainly is amazing deduction."

"Elementary," Meyer said grandly, and Bob O'Brien

stifled a laugh. "Let's look around, Bob. A rifle doesn't particularly strike me as the kind of weapon a woman would choose. What do you think?"

"I never think on Sundays," O'Brien said, but he began looking over the apartment. The place had a look of impermanence to it. There was a bed with brass bedstead against one wall, a night-table standing alongside it. A basin and a pitcher of water rested on the table. A floor lamp stood behind a worn easy chair in one corner of the room. A curtained closet was on the wall opposite the window. Beside that was the door leading to a tiny bathroom. O'Brien went into the bathroom and opened the medicine chest. It was empty. He pulled back the curtain on the closet and looked at the empty hangers.

"Whoever was here was traveling light," he remarked.

"Any signs of a woman?" Meyer said. "Lipstick tissues? Bobby pins? Long hairs?"

"Not even a sign of a human," O'Brien said. "Wait a minute, here's something." He lifted an ash tray from the night-table. "A cigar butt. Know any dames who smoke cigars?"

"Anne Baxter and Hermione Gingold," Meyer said. "Think they also fire rifles?"

"Maybe. But most actresses don't perform on Sundays. Besides, it would never be my luck to catch a case involving celebrities."

"I had a celebrity once," Meyer said. "A singer. It's a shame I was a married man at the time."

"Why?"

"Well," Meyer said, and he shrugged eloquently.

"It certainly is fascinating to watch you fellows at work," Pullen said.

"It beats television six ways from the middle," O'Brien said. "Most people think of cops as everyday workingmen who go to a musty office and type up reports in triplicate and do a lot of legwork all over the city. Just ordinary guys, you understand? Guys with wives and families. Guys like you and me, Mr. Pullen."

"Yes?" Pullen said.

"Sure. That's the influence of television. Actually, a detective is a pretty glamorous character. Ain't that right, Meyer?"

"Absolutely," Meyer said, sniffing the cigar butt.

"He's all the time getting involved with gorgeous blondes in slinky negligees. Ain't that right, Meyer?"

"Absolutely," Meyer said. The cigar was a White Owl. He made a mental note of it.

"He leads a life of gay adventurous excitement," O'Brien said. "When he ain't drinking in some very swank bar, he is out driving in a Cadillac convertible with the top down and the blonde's knees up on the seat. Boy, what a life! I'm telling you, Mr. Pullen, detective work ain't all routine."

"It sounds much more interesting than real estate," Pullen said.

"Oh, it is, it is. And the salary is fantastic." He winked. "Not to mention the graft. Mr. Pullen, don't believe what you see on television. Cops, Mr. Pullen, are not dull boobs."

"I never thought they were," Pullen said. "It certainly is fascinating the way you men work."

"You'd imagine somebody in the building would have heard a rifle going off twice, don't you think, Bob?" Meyer said.

"I would imagine so. Unless this is a home for the deaf."

"Any other apartments on this floor, Mr. Pullen?"

"There's one right across the hall," Pullen said. "I rented it myself."

"Let's try it, Bob."

They crossed the hall and knocked on the door. A young man in a short beard and a terry-cloth bathrobe opened it.

"Yo?" he said.

"Police," Meyer said. He flashed the tin.

"Man, dig the badge," the man in the bathrobe said.

"What's your name?" Meyer asked.

"Real or professional?"

"Both."

"Sid Lefkowitz is the square handle. When I'm on the stand, I use Sid Leff. Shorter, sweeter, and with a good beat."

"What stand?"

"The bandstand, man."

"You're a musician?"

"I blow guitar."

"Which name do you prefer?"

"Whichever one you like. I'm not choosy, man. Just blow your own ad lib chorus."

"Mr. Leff, did you hear any shots coming from the room across the hall?"

"Shots? Oh, is that what they were?"

"You heard them?"

"I heard something. But it didn't bother me. I was working on *Strings.*"

"On what?"

"*Symphony for Twelve Strings.* Don't get the wrong idea. It ain't from Bananasville. It's a jazz symphony. I'm writing it for three guitars, six violins, two bass fiddles, and a piano. The piano gets in by poetic license. What the hell, without the strings on the sounding board, there wouldn't be no piano, right?"

"Did you investigate the shots?"

"No. I figured them for backfires. Trucks go by here all the time. They take a short cut to the parkway through this street. A very noisy pad, this one. I'm thinking of busting out. How can a man concentrate in the midst of din, man, huh?"

"Did you happen to notice who was in that apartment?"

"The guy with the slush pump, you mean?"

"What?"

"The slush pump. The trombone. A guy came out of there with a trombone case under his arm."

"Anything else?"

"No. Just the horn."

"You saw the horn?"

"I saw the case. A guy wouldn't be carrying an empty trombone case would he? That's like carrying a guitar without strings. That would be a little too far out, man."

"Did you talk to him?"

"Exchanged a bit," Lefkowitz said. "The door was open when he passed by, and I spotted the horn case, and struck up a parley. He was going out on an afternoon wedding gig."

"A what?"

"A gig. A job. I told you, didn't I? The guy played trombone."

"What did he look like?"

"A big fellow with a busted nose. He had dark hair and dark eyes. He was smoking a cigar."

"Do you make him, Meyer?" O'Brien asked.

"Judging from the description on his record, it sounds like our man." He turned back to Lefkowitz. "Did he have a scar near his right eye?"

"I didn't get a good glim," Lefkowitz said. "He could have. I don't know."

"How do you know he was going to a wedding?"

"He said so. Said he was going on a wedding gig."

"He said he was going to play trombone at a wedding? Did he say that exactly?"

"No. He said he was going to a wedding. But why else would a guy take a horn to a wedding, if not to blow it?"

"What time was this?"

"I don't know. Close to five, I guess."

"All right. Thank you very much, Mr. Lefkowitz."

"Mine," Lefkowitz said.

"Huh?"

"The pleasure." He closed the door.

"What do you think?" O'Brien asked.

"Did you see a rifle in that first room?"

"No."

"And Lefkowitz said our boy was carrying nothing but a trombone case. Want a guess?"

"I outguess you already," O'Brien said. "There ain't a trombone in that case. There's a rifle."

"Yeah."

"And since there ain't no trombone, it's a cinch he ain't going to *play* at a wedding."

"Right."

"And if he's taking a rifle to a wedding, chances are —since he's already fired it twice—he plans to shoot it again."

"Right."

"And the only wedding I'm sure of today is Carella's sister's."

"Right."

"So let's head there."

"Does a guy walk into the middle of a reception with a rifle under his arm? A rifle isn't exactly a weapon you can conceal. Not after you take it out of that trombone case," Meyer said.

"So?"

"So I don't think he's heading for the wedding itself. I think maybe he's heading for someplace *near* the wedding. The same way he came to a place *near* the photography shop."

"And where might that be?" O'Brien asked.

"I haven't the faintest idea," Meyer said. "But how many men on the street are carrying trombone cases, would you suppose?"

"It certainly is fascinating the way you fellows work," Pullen said.

Christine Maxwell sat on the back porch of the Carella house, her hands moving nervously in her lap. Teddy Carella sat beside her, watching the dancers on the make-shift floor. The dancing was more frenetic now than it had been. Drinking had begun in earnest once the last course of the meal had been served. This was a wedding, a time for high celebration, and relatives from the far corners of the earth were out there on the floor whooping it up. The whooping up was causing consternation among many of the wives at the reception, but the consternation was tempered by the knowledge that this was a once-a-year day and that hasty kisses stolen from very distant cousins would hardly be remembered the next day. The only thing likely to be remembered the next day—when the gongs and hammers began to reverberate inside the skull—would be the fact that far too much liquor had been consumed the night before.

The children at the wedding reception had no problems at all, unless an overconsumption of soda pop could be considered a problem. This was better than an outing in the city park! This was better than a day at the circus! This was better than getting Captain Video's in-person autograph. For here was a dance floor to run around with gay abandon, slickly waxed, perfect for sliding and spill-ing. Here were grownups' legs to dodge between, here—in the case of the more precocious eleven-year-olds—were corseted behinds to pinch, a magnificent lawn to tear up. Oh, this was surely Heaven.

Christine Maxwell had no such illusions of Paradise. Sitting beside Teddy, she dreaded the moment when Steve Carella would begin questioning her. He didn't think *she'd* had anything to do with the old man's death, did he? No, he couldn't. Then why did he want to question her? The thought frightened her.

But more than that, she was frightened by the unex-pected jealousy exhibited by Cotton Hawes. She had willfully promoted the relationship with Jonesy in an attempt to bring Hawes to an appreciation of her obvious charms. Her little game had worked only too well. Hawes was not only annoyed, he was furious. And she did love him. She would not exchange him for a hundred Jonesys. Or a thousand.

"Oh, Teddy," she said, "what should I do?"

Teddy's face became instantly alert. The impression she gave of devoting her complete attention to whoever was speaking may have simply been an illusion. She was, after all, *forced* to watch a person's lips if she was to "hear" anything. But mechanical necessity did not explain the complete sympathy Teddy expressed as she listened. To the speaker, Teddy was a perfect sounding board. Her eyes, her mouth, her entire face took on a look of complete understanding. She tilted her head slightly now, and her eyebrows moved a fraction of an inch, the brown eyes focusing on Christine's mouth.

"I've made a mess of everything," Christine said, and Teddy leaned closer, watching the lips, nodding slightly to let Christine know she was listening.

"I haven't known Cotton very long," Christine said. "Oh, perhaps a year—but that isn't very long as relationships go. He came into my bookshop once, tracking down some typing paper which had been used in a warning note. I have a bookshop in Isola." She paused. "He asked me out, and I accepted. I've been seeing him." She paused again. "I'm a widow, you know. Not a Professional Widow, the way some girls are Professional Virgins or Professional Mothers. My husband was a pilot during the Second World War. He crashed over Okinawa. It took me a long time to get over it, but the dead are dead, and the living must go on. So I'm not a Professional Widow, Teddy. I haven't been wearing sackcloth and rolling about in the ashes. But . . . it was hard to fall in love again. It was hard to find any man who could live up to the memory of Greg. And then Cotton came along . . ."

Teddy nodded.

"And I fell in love again." She paused. "I don't think he loves me. In fact, I'm almost sure he doesn't. I really don't think Cotton is ready yet to become *really* involved with any woman. But I love him. And it's enough to be near him, and to be wanted by him. For now, that's enough." Again she paused. "I did a stupid thing today. I tried to make him jealous, and I think I may have lost him. Cotton isn't a man who can be pushed. Teddy, Teddy, what shall I do? What the hell shall I do?"

She fumbled for the purse in her lap as the tears sprang to her eyes. Snapping it open, she dug into it, expecting the familiar feel of her own bag, surprised when her hands struck something hard and unyielding. She stared into the purse.

A Smith & Wesson .357 Magnum stared back at her.

"They're on their way over, Steve," Kling said as he hung up the phone. "I explained the situation to them. They're coming in through the next street."

"Good," Carella said. He turned back to Sam Jones. "Now, let's do some serious talking, shall we, Jonesy?"

Jonesy nodded. His face was still white. His hands were still trembling in his lap.

"First of all, Jonesy, would you mind telling me where you went this afternoon when you left Tommy's house for your alleged walk?"

"Alleged?"

"Yes. Alleged. Where did you go?"

"Why?"

"Because somebody sawed through a rod connected to the steering tube of the Cadillac and we had an accident which damn near killed everybody in the car. That's why, Jonesy."

"I thought that accident—"

"*What* did you think?"

"I thought it was just an accident."

"It wasn't. And you were conveniently out of the car

at the time. Buying cigarettes, remember? Even though Tommy offered you his."

"You don't think . . ."

"All I want to know is where you went on your walk, that's all."

"I don't really remember. I was very nervous. I just walked."

"Where?"

"I came out of the house and walked. I must have walked about half a mile. Then I turned back."

"Meet anyone while you were walking?"

"No."

"Stop any place?"

"No."

"Then we have only your word for your whereabouts during the time that tie rod could have been sawed through."

"I suppose . . . if you put it that way . . ."

"How would *you* put it, Jonesy?"

"Why would I want to . . . why would I want to do a crazy thing like that?"

In a deadly flat voice, Carella said, "Tommy has a will leaving everything he owns to you."

"That? For Pete's sake, what the hell does he own?"

"What *does* he own, Jonesy?"

"How do I know? He's not a rich man, that's for sure. If he dies, there might be some money on his GI insurance policy. And he's got a 1958 Buick and probably a small savings account. But that's all that I know of."

"You seem to know an awful lot about it."

"Well, I'm his best friend. Why shouldn't I know? Besides, this isn't something a man would keep hidden. God, you don't think I'd try to kill Tommy—*Tommy!* My best friend!—for a few thousand dollars, do you?"

"It's been done for less," Carella said. "With best friends. With husbands and wives. With mothers and sons. Some people like money, Jonesy."

"Yeah, but . . . you're on the wrong track. I could never do a thing like that."

"There's Tommy's will."

"He's married now. He'll change that as soon as he comes back from his honeymoon."

"Which might be a damn good reason for killing him *now*," Kling said.

"Look, you guys are crazy," Jonesy said. "I wouldn't. I just *wouldn't* do a thing like that. You think I could kill Birnbaum? A nice old guy I've known since I was a kid? You think I could do a thing like that?"

"*Somebody* did a thing like that," Carella said.

"But not me. Why would I want to?" He paused and studied the detectives. "For Pete's sake, would I kill the only living witness to those wills? Does that make any sense to you?"

"He's got a point, Steve," Kling said.

"Look, I'm telling you," Jonesy said. "I had nothing to do with either Birnbaum's . . ."

There was a frantic knocking at the door. Christine Maxwell did not wait for anyone to open it. She threw it open and burst into the room waving the Magnum.

"I found this in my purse," she said. "Not my purse. A girl took mine by accident. In the ladies' room. She left this one. I thought it was . . ."

"Slow down," Carella said.

". . . my bag, and I opened it to get a hanky, and this was inside." She waved the gun again.

"Stop waving that damn thing, it may be loaded!" Carella shouted, and he took the gun from her. Then he nodded. "This is it, Bert," he said. He sniffed the barrel. "We won't have to look any further for the gun that killed Birnbaum." He turned to Christine. "You said this was in your purse?"

"No. I only thought it was my purse. A blond girl was in the ladies' room with me. She must have taken my bag by mistake. She left this one."

"A blonde?" Kling said.

"Yes."

"What did she look like?"

"A very big girl," Christine said, "in a red silk dress."

"Ouch!" Kling said. "I was *dancing* with her before dinner."

"Let's find her," Carella said, and he started for the door.

"She's probably a million miles . . ." Kling started, and at that moment Tommy Giordano came breathlessly into the bedroom.

"Steve!" he said. "Steve, I'm . . . I'm going out of my mind with worry."

"What is it?" Carella asked.

"It's Angela! I can't find her anywhere. She's gone!"

Chapter 11

THERE WAS THE STRONG smell of cigar smoke.

There was a long shaft of light far away, and a silhouette filling the piercing beam.

There was pain, excruciating pain which throbbed and vibrated and sang with a thousand shrill voices.

There was warmth, a warmth that was thick and liquidy, oozing, oozing.

Cotton Hawes fought unconsciousness.

He felt as if his body was quivering. He felt as if every part of him was swinging in a wild circle of nauseating blackness. Some inner sense told him he was lying flat on his back, and yet he had the feeling that his hands were clutching, grasping, trying to reach something in the blackness, as if his legs and feet were twitching uncontrollably. The pain at the side of his face was unbearable. It was the pain, finally, which forced away the unconsciousness, needling him with persistent fire, forcing sensibility into his mind, and then his body. He blinked.

The cigar smell was overpowering. It filled his newly alert nostrils with the stink of a thousand saloons. The shaft of light was penetrating and merciless, flowing steadily through an open window at the end of the room, impaling him with sunshine. A man stood at the window, his back to Hawes.

Hawes tried to get to his feet, and the nausea came back with frightening suddenness, swimming into his head and then dropping like a swirling stone to the pit of his stomach. He lay still, not daring to move, aware now that the side of his face was bleeding, remembering now the sudden blinding blow that had knocked him to the floor unconscious. The nausea passed. He could feel the steady seeping of the blood as it traveled past his jawbone and onto his neck. He could almost feel each separate drop of blood rolling over his flesh to be sopped up instantly by the white collar of his shirt. He felt as if he were being born, hypersensitive to every nuance of smell, and sight, and touch. And, newborn, he was also weak. He knew he could not stand without falling flat on his face.

He turned his head slightly to the left. He could see the man at the window clearly, each part of the man combining with the next to form a sharply defined portrait of power as he crouched by the window, the late afternoon sunshine enveloping the silhouette in whitish licking flames of light.

The man's hair was black, worn close to his skull in a tight-fitting woolly cap. The man's brow was immense in profile, a hooked nose jutting out from bushy eyebrows pulled into a frown. A small scar stood out in painful relief against the tight skin of the man's face, close to the right eye. The man's mouth was a tight, almost lipless line that gashed deep into the face above a jaw cleft like a horse's buttocks. His neck was thick, and his shoulders bulged beneath the blue tee shirt he wore, biceps rolling hugely into thick forearms covered with black hair that resembled steel wool. One huge hand was clutched around the barrel of a rifle. The rifle, Hawes noticed, was mounted with a telescopic sight. An open box of cartridges rested near the man's right shoe.

This is no one to tangle with in my present condition, Hawes thought. This may be no one to tangle with in any condition. He looks like a man who tears telephone books in sixteenths. He looks like a man who allows automobiles to drive over his inflated chest. He looks like the meanest son of a bitch I have ever seen in my life, and I am not anxious to tangle with him. Now, or maybe never.

But that's a rifle he's holding, and it has a telescopic sight, and he sure as hell doesn't plan to pick his teeth with it.

Do I still have my gun? Or has he disarmed me?

Hawes looked down the length of his nose. He could see the white throat of his shirt stained with blood. He could see his shoulder holster strapped to his chest beneath his open coat.

The holster was empty.

There's nothing I can do but lie here, he thought, and wait for my strength to come back.

And pray, meanwhile, that he doesn't take a pot shot at anybody across the yard at the reception.

The black MG convertible had been a gift from Ben Darcy's parents. Unaware of his private intention to enter dental school, they had offered the sleek, low-slung car to him as a sort of bribe. Ben had accepted the bribe and then entered dental school, anyway, just as he'd planned to. Everybody was happy.

The car was capable of hitting rather high speeds on a straight run, and Ben was doing his best at the moment to prove that the manufacturer's claims were valid. The top down, his foot jammed on the accelerator, he cruised along Semplar Parkway at the low-flying speed of eighty-five miles an hour.

Beside him, her long brown hair blowing back over her shoulders, Angela Giordano, nee Angela Carella, watched the road ahead with wide eyes, certain she would be killed on her wedding day.

"Ben, can't you slow down?" she pleaded.

"I like to drive fast," he answered. "Angela, you've got to listen to me."

"I'm listening, Ben, but I'm scared. If another car should . . ."

"Don't worry about me!" he snapped. "I'm the best damn driver in Riverhead. You couldn't be in better hands."

"All right, Ben," she said, and she clutched her hands in her lap and swallowed hard and continued to watch the road.

"So you married him," Ben said.

"Yes."

"Why?"

"Oh, Ben, really, we went through all this on the dance floor. I wouldn't have come with you if I'd known . . ."

"Why *did* you come with me?" he asked quickly.

"Because you said you wanted to take me for a spin for the last time. A ride around the block, you said. All right, I believed you. But we're *not* going around the block, we're on the parkway heading toward the next state, and you're driving much too fast. *Ben, would you please slow down?*"

"No," he said. "Why'd you marry him?"

"Because I love him. Does that answer you?"

"I don't believe you."

"Believe me. Please believe me."

"I don't. How can you be in love with him? A bank clerk! For the love of God, Angela, he's a bank clerk!"

"I love him."

"What can he offer you? What's he ever going to give you?"

"He doesn't have to give me anything," Angela said. "I love him."

"I'm better-looking than he is," Ben said.

"Maybe you are."

"I'm going to be a dentist."

"Yes."

"Why'd you marry *him?*"

"Ben, please, please slow down. I'm . . ." Her eyes widened. "Ben! Look out!"

The Buick came hurtling onto Ben's side of the parkway suddenly, passing a slower car ahead of it. It came like a steam locomotive, unable to cut back because of the car ahead, committed to the pass, determined to reach the safety of its own lane by a new burst of speed. Ben recognized the impossibility of the situation. He swung the wheel sharply to the right, heading for the grass at the side of the parkway. The Buick *whooshed* past with the roar of a diving jet as the small MG cleared the vented fender of the bigger car by no more than a foot, climbing onto the steeply sloping bank of grass, and then executing a small sharp turn to the left as Ben yanked the wheel over again. For a moment, Angela thought the car would roll over. Tires squealed as it hit the concrete again, going into a skid, and then straightening to face the dead center arrow of the parkway. Ben slammed his foot onto the accelerator. The speed indicator rose to 90.

Angela could not speak. She sat beside him gasping for breath. And finally she closed her eyes. She would not watch. She *could* not watch.

"It's still not too late," Ben said.

His voice droned in her ears over the rush of air in the open cockpit of the sports car. Her eyes were closed, and his voice sounded strange, low and meaningful, droning on monotonously.

"It's still not too late. You can still get out of it. You can have it annulled. He's wrong for you, Angela. You'd find that out, anyway. Get rid of him, Angela. Angela, I love you. You can have it annulled."

She shook her head, her eyes closed tightly.

"Don't go on the honeymoon, Angela. Don't go with him. Tell him you've made a mistake. It's not too late. You'd be doing the right thing. Otherwise . . ."

She shook her head again. Weakly, she murmured, "Ben, take me back."

"I'll be waiting for you, Angela. Get rid of him. He's no good for you. Do it yourself, Angela. Tell him, tell him."

"Ben, take me back," she mumbled. "Please take me back. Please. Please. Please please please please please . . ."

"Will you tell him? Will you tell him you want it annulled?"

"Ben, please please . . ."

"Will you?"

"Yes," she said. "I'll tell him." She did not care that she was lying. She only wanted the nightmare of this ride to end, wanted to get away from the man beside her. "Yes," she lied again, and then she gave the lie strength and conviction. "Yes, take me back and I'll tell him. Take me back, Ben."

"I don't believe you. You're not really going to tell him."

"I am!"

"Do you love me?"

She could not answer.

"Do you love me?"

"No," she said, and she began weeping bitterly. "I love Tommy, I love Tommy! Why are you doing this to me, Ben? Why are you torturing me like this? If you ever cared anything for me, take me back! Please take me back!"

"All right," he snapped suddenly. He slowed the car, and then executed a screeching U-turn. His foot pressed against the accelerator once more. Angela did not look at the speedometer.

Tommy was waiting at the curb when the MG pulled up before the Carella house. Angela leaped from the car and rushed into his arms, and he held her for a moment and then said, "What the hell's the idea, Ben?"

"It was just a wedding gag," Ben said, grinning feebly. "Kidnaping the bride, you know? Just a gag."

"You've got one hell of a sense of humor. You're lucky I don't knock you flat on your ass. You had us all going nuts here until we noticed your car was gone. God-damnit, Ben, I don't think this is the least bit funny. I don't think it's funny at all. Goddamnit, I think I *will* knock you on your ass!"

"Come on, where's your sense of humor?" Ben said, and again he grinned feebly.

"Oh, go to hell, you bastard," Tommy answered. He put his arm around Angela. "Come on, honey, let's go inside."

"You want me to go home?" Ben asked sheepishly.

"Go, stay, do what you want. Just keep away from Angela."

"I was only kidding," Ben said.

The men surrounding the body of Birnbaum the neighbor were not kidding at all. There was something very unfunny about murder. No matter when it happened, or where, it was still uncomical. There were some who maintained that the worst murders were those which dragged a man out in the wee hours of the morning. There were others who despised early evening murders. But each murder seemed the worst when it was happening, and each of the men who stood looking down at Birnbaum's lifeless shape agreed—though they did not voice it—that the worst time to be killed was in the late afternoon.

The 112th Squad had sent one detective over because the murder had been committed within its boundaries and because the case would officially be theirs from here on in. Homicide, informed that four bona fide detectives were at the scene, decided not to send anyone over. But a police photographer was taking pictures of the corpse fastidiously, if without the energetic grasshopperiness of a Jody Lewis. The assistant medical examiner was officially pronouncing Birnbaum dead and instructing the stretcher bearers on how to carry him out to the meat wagon waiting next to the curb in front of Birnbaum's house. Some boys from the lab had put in an appearance, too, and they were attempting now to find foot imprints from which they could make a cast. All in all, everyone was pretty busy compiling the statistics of sudden and violent death. Unfortunately, none of the investigators felt the need to make a telephone call. Had the need presented itself, one or another of the men might have wandered into the Birnbaum house which stood forty feet from the shielding line of shrubbery behind which they worked.

In the attic of the Birnbaum house, Cotton Hawes felt his strength returning. For the past ten minutes, he had lain silently, his eyes flicking from one corner of the attic to another, and then back to the patiently waiting powerhouse squatting on the floor near the window. The attic was filled with the discarded paraphernalia of living: bundles of old magazines, a green trunk marked "CAMP IDLEMERE" in white paint, a dressmaker's dummy, a lawn mower without blades, a hammer, an Army duffel bag, a radio with a smashed face, three albums marked "Photographs" and numerous other items which had undoubtedly cluttered the busy life of a family.

The only item which interested Hawes was the hammer.

It rested on top of the trunk some four feet from where he lay.

If he could get the hammer without being heard or seen, he would promptly use it on the sniper's skull. Provided the sniper didn't turn first and shoot him. It would not be too pleasant to get shot at close range with a rifle.

Well, when? Hawes asked himself.

Not now. I'm not strong enough yet.

You're never going to get any stronger, Hawes thought. *Are you afraid of that big bastard crouched by the window?*

Yes.

What?

Yes, I'm afraid of him. He can break me in half even without using his rifle. And he may use it. So I'm afraid of him, and the hell with you.

Let's go, coward, Hawes thought. *Let's make our play for the hammer. There's no time like the present, the man said.*

The man didn't have to face Neanderthal.

Look, are we . . . ?

All right, all right, let's go.

Silently, he rolled over onto his side. The sniper did not turn. He rolled again, completing a full turn this time, coming to rest a foot away from the trunk. Swallowing hard, he reached out for the hammer. Soundlessly, he slid it off the trunk and gripped it tightly in his right hand.

He swallowed again and got to his knees.

Okay, he thought, we rush him now, hammer raised. We crease his skull before he knows what hit him.

Ready?

He got to a crouching position.

Set?

He stood up and raised the hammer high.

Go!

He took a step forward.

The door behind him opened suddenly.

"Hold it, mister!" a voice said, and he whirled to face

a big blonde in a red silk dress. She was reaching into her purse as he leaped at her.

Chapter 12

IT CANNOT BE SAID of Cotton Hawes that he did not ordinarily enjoy wrestling with blondes whose proportions matched this one's. For here was truly a blonde. Here was a handful, and an armful, and an eyeful; here was the image which automatically came to mind whenever anyone muttered the magic words "big blonde."

Standing on a runway in Union City, this girl would have caused heart stoppage. Third-row bald heads would have turned pale with trembling.

On the legitimate Broadway stage, this girl would have set the theater on fire, set the customers on their ears, and set the critics rushing back to their typewriters to pound out ecstatic notices.

In a bedroom—Hawes's imagination reeled with the thought.

But unfortunately, this girl was not on a runway or a stage or a bed. This girl was standing in the doorway to a room no bigger than an upper berth in a Pullman. This girl was obviously not planning to set anyone but Hawes on his ear. She reached into her purse with all the determination of a desert rat digging for water, and then her hand stopped, and a surprised look came over her lovely features. In clear, crystal-pure, ladylike tones, she yelled, "Where's my goddamn gun?" and Hawes leaped on her.

The sniper turned from the window at the same moment.

The girl was all flesh and a yard wide. She was also all

teeth and all nails. She clamped two rows of teeth into Hawes's hand as he struggled for a grip, and then her nails flashed out wildly, raking the uninjured half of his face. The sniper circled closer, shouting, "Get away from him, Oona! I can't do anything with you . . ."

Hawes did not want to hit the girl. He especially did not want to hit her with the hammer. But the hammer was the only weapon he possessed and he reasoned correctly that if this girl got away from him, Neanderthal would either club him into the floorboards with the stock of the rifle or, worse, plunk a few slugs into his chest. Neither prospect seemed particularly entertaining. The blonde herself was not entertaining in the slightest. Wiggling in his arms, she delivered a roundhouse punch which almost knocked out his right eye. He winced in pain and swung at her with the hammer, but she ducked inside the blow and brought her knee to his groin in an old trick she'd probably learned in grammar school, so expertly did she execute it. Hawes had been kicked before. He'd also been kicked in the groin before. His reactions, he discovered, were always the same. He always doubled over in pain. But this time, as he doubled, he clutched at the blonde because the blonde was insurance. As long as her hot little body remained close to his, the sniper was helpless. He clutched at her, and he caught the front of her dress and it gave under his hand, tearing in a long rip which exposed the blonde's white brassiere and three-quarters of her left breast.

The material kept ripping, with the blonde at the end of it like an unraveling ball of wool in the paws of a playful kitten. He swung the hammer again, catching her on the shoulder, stopping her movement, clutching again, catching flesh this time, his fingers closing tightly as he pulled her toward him. The blonde's dress was torn to the waist now, but Hawes wasn't interested in anatomy. Hawes was interested in clubbing her with the hammer. He swung her around, and her backside came up hard against him, a solid muscular backside. He swung one arm around her neck, his elbow cushioned between the fleshy mounds of the girl's breasts, and he brought back the hand with the hammer again, and the girl pulled another old grammar school trick.

She bent suddenly from the knees, and then shot upward with the force of a piston, the top of her skull slamming into Hawes's jaw. His arm dropped. The girl swung around and leaped at him, a nearly bare-breasted fury, clawing at his eyes. He swung the hammer. It struck her right arm, and she clutched at it in pain, her face distorted. "You son of a bitch!" she said, and she reached down, her knee coming up, her skirt pulling back over legs which would have been magnificent on the French Riviera stemming from a bikini, and then she pulled off one high-heeled pump and came at Hawes with the shoe clutched like a mace.

"Get the hell away from him!" the sniper yelled, but the girl would not give up the fight. Circling like wrestlers, the girl's chest heaving in the barely restraining brassiere, Hawes panting breathlessly, one holding a hammer, the other a spiked-heeled shoe, they searched for an opening. The girl's lips were skinned back over teeth which looked as if they could bite Hawes in two.

She feinted with the shoe, and he brought up his left arm to ward off the blow, and then she moved swiftly to one side, and he saw only the blur of the red shoe coming at his face, felt only the crashing pain as the stiletto-like spike hit his temple. He felt his fingers loosen from the handle of the hammer. He felt himself pitching forward. He held out his arms to stop his fall, and the girl caught him as he came toward her and his head bounced against her shoulder, slid, and he felt the warm cushion of her breast for an instant before she viciously pushed him away from her.

He struck the floor and the last shamed thought he had was *A girl. Jesus, a girl . . .*

A boy or a girl, the baby was kicking up a storm.

Sitting with her father-in-law who had surely had too much to drink, Teddy Carella could not remember the heir apparent ever having raised such a fuss.

It was difficult for her to appreciate the oncoming dusk with her son- or daughter-to-be doing his early-evening calisthenics. Every now and then the baby would kick her sharply, and she'd start from the sudden blow, certain that everyone at the reception was witnessing her wriggling fidgets. The baby seemed to have a thousand feet, God forbid! He kicked her high in the belly, close under her breasts, and then he kicked her again, lower in the pelvic region, and she was sure he'd turned a somersault, so widely diverse had the kicks been.

It'll be over next week, she thought, and she sighed. No more backaches. No more children pointing fingers at me in the street. *Hey, lady, what time does the balloon go up?* Ha-ha, very funny. She glanced across the dance floor. The redhead from Teaneck or Gowanus or wherever had latched onto a new male, but it hadn't helped Teddy very much. Steve hadn't been anywhere near for the past few hours, and she wondered now what it was that could possibly be keeping him so occupied. Of course, it was his sister's wedding, and she supposed he was duty bound to play the semi-host. But why had Tommy called him so early this morning? And what where Bert and Cotton doing here? With the instincts of a cop's wife, she knew that something was in the wind—but she didn't know quite what.

The baby kicked her again.

Damn, she thought, I do wish you'd stop that.

Tony Carella had drunk a lot of whisky and a lot of wine and a lot of champagne. He had not drunk so much since the time Steve got married and that was years ago.

In the glow of his stupor, he began to like the Weddings–Fetes, Incorporateds. They were really nice fellows.

It was worth all the money he was giving them. Oh, *madonna*, how much money he was giving them! But it was worth it. Every penny. They were nice boys, all of them. Look at the nice dance floor they had made, bringing in that big flat platform and laying it right down in the center of his lawn, *Santa Maria*, my lawn! But they were nice boys. Look at the nice thing they had built for the fireworks at the end of the property. They would be nice, the fireworks. He loved the Weddings–Fetes, Incorporateds. He loved his wife. He loved his son and his daughter-in-law, and his daughter and his son-in-law. He loved everybody.

He loved Birnbaum.

Where was Birnbaum, anyway?

Why wasn't Birnbaum sitting next to him on this day of his joy, drinking wine and champagne? If he knew Birnbaum, the old man was probably off in a corner someplace weeping.

My old friend, Tony thought, weeping.

I will find him. I will find him and give him a cigar.

He was starting out of his chair when he heard the scream from the edge of his property.

Carella had dispatched the boys from the 112th, the photographer, the assistant medical examiner, and the laboratory assistants, wondering all the while where Cotton Hawes had gone. He'd asked Cotton to stay with the body. Well, the body was now gone—and nearly everyone concerned with the body was also gone. And so was Cotton.

But where?

He had not been working with Hawes for too long a time, but he felt certain the man would not have pulled a stunt so childish as walking out on his date. Still, he'd been pretty angry back there a little while ago. And Christine, as cute as she was, had certainly been asking for trouble. She'd wanted Cotton to do a burn, and he had, but she'd stumbled onto a corpse in the bargain, which proves you shouldn't play with fire, girls.

But would Cotton have walked out on her?

It was possible. Carella had to concede that it was definitely possible. There was no second-guessing the ways of maids and men. He'd handled many a suicide where a seemingly levelheaded young man had thrown himself out the nearest hotel window because a sweet young thing in a skirt had refused a date. Why, take his own Teddy. Annoyed because he'd been dancing with that wench from Flemington. God, that had been a long time ago, he could remember every detail of that night as if it were happening now. Faye, grrrr, she'd been a wonderful, wonderful . . .

Hey now.

Steady, lad.

He saw Teddy sitting near his father. He grinned and began walking toward her.

From the woods behind him, he heard someone scream, "Help! Help!"

He whirled and broke into a trot, crashing into the bushes. His service revolver was in his fist before he'd covered three feet.

The boys had been standing on the corner watching all the girls go by. They had been standing there all afternoon, they said. They had been standing right under that same lamppost near the el structure. Just standing. Just watching the girls. June was a good time for watching the girls, the boys said.

"Did you happen to notice the people who came down off the train?" Meyer asked.

"Yeah, we noticed the girls," the boys said.

"Did you notice anybody else?"

"Yeah," the boys said, "but mostly we noticed the girls."

"Did you happen to see a man carrying a trombone case?"

"What does a trombone case look like?"

"You know," O'Brien said. "A trombone case. Black leather. Long. With a sort of a flaring bell on one end."

"Gee," the boys said. "You'd better ask Charlie."

"Which one of you is Charlie?"

"Charlie's in the candy store. Hey, Charlie! Charlie, come on out here!"

"Is Charlie a musician?" Meyer asked.

"No, but his sister is taking piano lessons. She's eight years old."

"How old is Charlie?" Meyer asked skeptically.

"Oh, he's a grown man," the boys said. "He's sixteen."

Charlie came out of the candy store. He was a thin boy with a crew cut. He wore khaki trousers and a white tee shirt, and he ambled over to the boys under the lamppost with a curious expression on his face.

"Yeah!" he said.

"These guys have some questions."

"Yeah!" He delivered the word as a cross between a question and an exclamation, as if surprised by his own query.

"Do you know what a trombone case looks like, Charlie?"

"Yeah!" he said, and again it was both a question and an exclamation.

"Did you see anyone come down those steps carrying one?"

"A *trombone* case?" This time it was purely a question.

"Yes," Meyer said.

"Today?"

"Yes."

"Down those steps?"

"Yes."

"Yeah!" he said, the exclamation preceding the question.

"Which way did he go?"

"How do I know?" Charlie said.

"You saw him, didn't you?"

"Yeah! Why? You need a trombone player? Does it have to be a trombone player? My kid sister plays piano."

"Think, Charlie. Which way did he go?"

"Who remembers? You think I followed him or something?"

"He came down those steps?"

"Yeah!"

"Did he turn right or left?"

Charlie thought for a moment. "Neither," he said at last. "He walked straight up the avenue."

"And then what?"

"I don't know."

"Did he turn at the corner?"

"I don't know."

"You lost him after he walked past that corner?"

"I don't know whether he walked past that corner or not. Who lost him? I wasn't even trying to find him. Who was interested in him?"

"Do you think he passed that corner?"

"I don't know."

"Do you think he turned at the corner?"

"I don't know."

"Could he have crossed the street?"

"I'm telling you, *I don't know.*" He paused. "Listen, why don't you ask the guy in the delly on the next corner. Maybe he seen him."

"Thanks, son," Meyer said, "we'll do that."

"I'm sorry," Charlie said. "Does it have to be a trombone player?"

"I'm afraid so."

" 'Cause my kid sister plays some gone piano, I mean it." Meyer looked at Charlie sadly. Charlie shrugged. "So some guys go for horns," he said resignedly, and he went back into the candy store.

Meyer and O'Brien started up the avenue.

"What do you think?" O'Brien said.

"Sounds as if it might be him. Who knows? Maybe we'll have some luck in the delicatessen."

They did not have any luck in the delicatessen.

The man behind the counter wore bifocals, had been busy all day waiting on Sunday customers, and wouldn't have known a trombone case from a case of crabs, good day.

Meyer and O'Brien went out onto the sidewalk.

"Where to?"

Meyer shook his head. "Boy," he said, "this suddenly seems like a very big neighborhood."

Chapter 13

BEN DARCY LAY ON HIS back in the bushes.

Dusk was coming on, staining the sky with purple. In the woods, the insects were beginning their night song. The city looked skyward and greeted the impending night with a sigh; this was Sunday and tomorrow was another workday. And in the city, in the imposing steel and concrete structures of Isola, in the teeming streets of Calm's Point, in the suburban outlands of Riverhead, the beginning of night seemed to bring with it a touch of peace, a restfulness which bordered on weary resignation. Another day was moving into the coolness of the past. The moon would rise, and stars would pepper the skies, and the city would suddenly be ablaze with light.

Ben Darcy seemed to be a part of the peacefulness of dusk. Lying on his back on the ground beneath the big maple which dominated the surrounding area of bushes, he looked like nothing more than a summer sleeper, a dreamer, a sky-watcher, the classic boy with the strand of straw between his teeth. His arms were outstretched. His eyes were closed. He seemed to be asleep, at peace with himself and with the world.

The top of his skull was bleeding.

Stooping down beside him quickly, Carella saw the cut at once, and his fingers moved to it rapidly, parting the hair, feeling the swelling around the gash. The cut was not a deep one or a long one, nor did it bleed profusely. It sat in the exact center of Darcy's skull, and the area surrounding it had swelled to the size of a walnut. In the growing darkness, Steve Carella sighed audibly. He was tired, very tired. He did not enjoy chasing specters. I should have been a prizefighter, he thought. A good dirty sport where the combat is clearly stated from go, where the rules are set down by an impartial observer, where the arena is circumscribed from the very beginning, where the opponent is plainly visible and plainly identified as the opponent, the only man to beat, the only enemy.

Why the hell would anyone ever choose police work as his profession, he wondered.

We're dealing with destruction, he thought, and the destruction is always secret and our job is not so much preventing it as it is discovering it after it has happened. We seek out the destroyers, but this doesn't make us creators because we are involved in a negative task, and creation is never a negative act. Teddy, sitting out there, with a baby inside her, creating with no effort, creating by nature, is accomplishing more than I'll accomplish in fifty years of police work. Why would anyone ever want to get involved with a son of a bitch who saws through the tie rods of an automobile or kills the neighbor, Birnbaum, or takes a whack at the skull of Darcy? Why would anyone choose as his profession, as the job to which he devotes most of his waking hours, a task which must necessarily bring him into contact with the destroyers?

Why would anyone deliberately involve himself in the murky, involuted motivational processes of the criminal mind, dirty his hands with the crawling specimens of humanity who parade into that squadroom every day of the week, every week of the year?

Why would anyone want to become a street cleaner?

I will tell you some things, Steve, he thought.

I will tell you first that philosophy is unbecoming to a cop who almost flunked Philosophy I in school.

I will tell you secondly that free choice is something which is very rarely offered to human beings. You became a cop because you became a cop, and you couldn't tell yourself why without spending hours on a head shrinker's couch, and even then you might not know. And you remain a cop—why?

Because—discounting the obvious knowledge that a man must feed and clothe his wife and his family, discounting any insecurities about facing the world outside the police department, scrounging for a job when I'm no longer a boy, discounting any of this—I *want* to be a cop.

Not because *someone* has to clean the streets. Maybe no one has to clean the streets at all. Maybe civilization would move along just as briskly if the streets were filthy as hell.

But the destroyers make me angry. When the destroyers take life from a man like Birnbaum, they make me mad as hell! And so long as destruction makes me angry, I'll continue to be a cop, I'll continue commuting to a scroungy squadroom in perhaps the world's worst neighborhood, listening to bum jokes delivered by other cops, listening to corny humor, and telephones ringing, and complaints from the gentle people who—though they may not all be creators—are *not* destroyers.

In the deepening darkness, he grinned wanly.

You may not have realized it, Father Paul, he thought,

but you had a very religious man in your rectory today.

He left Ben Darcy lying on his back, and he went to the house for some water and some damp rags.

The wedding jokes were beginning.

Standing before the long bridal table upon which rested the trays of *dolci* and the huge wedding cake and—at the far end—two bottles of wine marked separately and respectively for the bride and the groom, Tommy listened to the wedding jokes with mixed feelings. He was embarrassed by them, but he was also secretly pleased by them. He knew he was supposed to be embarrassed by them, but he was also secretly pleased by them. He knew he was supposed to be embarrassed and so each new joke brought a flush to his boyish features. But at the same time, he secretly felt as if he had achieved manhood at last. Finally, he was being granted admission to a worldwide fraternity as a junior member. Years from now, perhaps, he would attend someone else's wedding and tell the same ritual jokes. The knowledge pleased him, even though he'd heard most of the jokes before. The jokes had started with that hoary old standby of the man who leaves his umbrella in a hotel room which is later occupied by a honeymoon couple. About to retrieve the umbrella as they enter the room, he ducks into a closet and is forced to listen to their cooing lovemaking. Finally in desperation, after listening to the groom asking the bride questions like "And whose eyes are these?"—"*Yours, darling*"—"And whose lovely lips are these?"—"*Yours, sweetheart*"—on and on, sparing no part of the anatomy, the joke tinged with the delicious unsavoriness of total possession and the anticipation of an outer-directed strip tease, the man in the closet shouts, "When you get to the umbrella, it's *mine!*"

Tommy laughed. The joke had a beard, but he laughed anyway, and he blushed slightly, and he watched his brother-in-law emerge from the bushes at the side of the property and rush toward the house, and then another joke started, the one about the midget who marries the circus fat lady, and this was followed by another, and then another, and then the jokes left the realm of scripted humor and took on an ad lib quality, each prankster, both married man and bachelor, coming up with top-of-the-head advice on the proper hotel-room behavior. Someone threw in the hoary story about the white horse who married a zebra and spent the entire honeymoon trying to take off her striped pajamas, and Tommy laughed, and someone advised him to bring along a lot of magazines because Angela would undoubtedly spend three hours in the bathroom preparing herself for the biggest moment of her life, and someone else said, "He only wishes it were the *biggest* moment," and though Tommy didn't quite get this one, he laughed anyway.

"What hotel are you going to, Tom?" one of the circle of jokesters asked.

"Uh-uh," Tommy said, shaking his head.

"Come on!" someone shouted. "You don't think we'd barge in on your honeymoon, do you?"

"I do," Tommy said.

"Old pals like us? Don't you *want* us to visit you?"

"No!"

"No? Why not? Have you made other plans for this evening?"

And so it went. And all the while, Jody Lewis scampered around the circle of jokesters, catching the expression on Tommy's face each time a new joke was told, the shutter clicking, clicking, to preserve the blush or the grin or the fleeting look of realized manhood for posterity, *Our Wedding Day.*

"Don't forget that wine when you leave!" someone shouted.

"What wine?"

"Somebody brought you wine. At the end of the table. One for the bride and one for the groom."

"But don't drink too much, Tommy. Too much wine, and you're going to have a very disappointed bride!"

"Just a sip, Tommy! A toast! And then to work!"

The crowd laughed. Jody Lewis kept his shutter clicking. Night was falling with a frightening rush.

Oona Blake crouched on the floor over Cotton Hawes, her skirt pulled back over powerfully beautiful legs, the top of her dress torn to the waist. Darkness had invaded the small attic room of the Birnbaum house. The vanishing light of daytime filtered feebly through the attic window, catching her blond hair and then the white exposed flank of her thigh as she knotted the ropes securely around Hawes's body and then went through his pockets.

Marty Sokolin, chewing on his cigar, one huge hand around the rifle barrel, watched her. She scared him somewhat. She was the most beautiful girl he'd ever known in his life, but she moved with the power of a Nike rocket, and she scared him sometimes; but she excited him, too. Watching her flip open the man's wallet, watching her hands as they quickly went through the contents, he was frightened and excited.

"A cop," she said.

"How do you know?"

"A badge, and an ID card. Why didn't you search him before?"

"I was too busy. What's a cop doing here? How'd a cop . . . ?"

"They're crawling all over the place," Oona said.

"Why?" His eyes blinked. He bit down more fiercely on the cigar.

"I shot a man," she answered, and he felt a tiny lurch of fear.

"You . . . ?"

"I shot a man, an old fart who was heading for this house. You told me to keep people away from here, didn't you?"

"Yes, but to *shoot* a man! Oona, why'd you . . . ?"

"Aren't you *here* to shoot a man?"

"Yes, but . . ."

"Did you want someone coming up here?"

"No, Oona, but it's brought cops. I've got a record, for Christ's sake. I can't . . ."

"So have I," she snapped, and he watched the sudden fury in her eyes, and again he was frightened. Sweat erupted on his upper lip. In the gathering gloom, he watched her, frightened, excited.

"Do you want to kill Giordano?" she said.

"Yes. I . . . I do."

"Do you or don't you?"

"I don't know. Jesus, Oona, I don't know. I don't want cops. I don't want to go to jail again."

"That's not what you told me."

"I know, I know."

"You said you wanted him dead."

"Yes."

"You said you'd never be able to rest until he was dead."

"Yes."

"You asked for my help. I gave it to you. Without me, you wouldn't know how to wipe your nose. Who got the apartment near the photography shop? Me. Who suggested this house? Me. Without me, you'd be carrying your goddamn grudge to the grave. Is that what you want? To carry the grudge to your grave?"

"No, Oona, but . . ."

"Are you a man . . . or what are you?"

"I'm a man."

"You're nothing. You're afraid to shoot him, aren't you?"

"No."

"I've already killed for you, do you know that? I've already killed a man to protect you. And now you're chickening out. What are you? A man or what?"

"I'm a man!" Sokolin said.

"You're nothing. I don't know why I took up with you. I could have had men, real men. You're not a man."

"I'm a man!"

"Then kill him!"

"Oona! It's just . . . there are cops now. There's a cop *here,* right with us . . ."

"There'll be fireworks at eight o'clock . . ."

"Oona, if I kill him, what do I accomplish? I know I said I . . ."

". . . a lot of noise, a lot of explosions. If you fire then, the shot won't even be heard. No one will hear it."

". . . wanted him dead, but now I don't know. Maybe he wasn't responsible for Artie's getting shot. Maybe he didn't know . . ."

"You go to the window, Marty. You pick him up in your sights."

". . . there was a sniper in the trees. I'm clean now. I'm out of jail. Why should I fool around with something like this?"

"You wait for the fireworks to start. You squeeze the trigger. He's dead, and we take off."

"And the cop laying there on the floor? He's seen both of us," Sokolin protested.

"I'll take care of him," Oona Blake said, and she grinned. "It'll be a real pleasure to take care of him." Her voice dropped to a whisper. "Get to the window, Marty."

"Oona . . ."

"Get to the window and get it over with. As soon as the fireworks start. Get it over and done with. And then come with me, Marty, come with me, baby, come to Oona, baby, Marty, get it over with, get it over with, *get it out of your system!*"

"Yes," he said. "Yes, Oona."

Antonio Carella had perhaps drunk too much wine,

or danced too strenuously. In any case, he was having difficulty standing. He had carried a chair to the center of the dance floor, and he stood on the chair now, wobbling unsteadily, his arms flailing the air, and he tried to maintain his balance and signal for silence simultaneously. The weddng guests had also drunk too much—perhaps —or perhaps danced too strenuously. They were a long time coming to silence and perhaps they never would have were it not for the fear that Tony Carella would fall off that chair unless someone began listening to him soon.

"I'm a very lucky man today," Tony said to the hushed guests. "My daughter Angela has married a wonderful boy. Tommy! Tommy? Where's Tommy?"

He climbed down off the chair and searched for Tommy in the crowd, dragging him into the light that spilled from the bandstand.

"My son-in-law!" he shouted, and the wedding guests applauded. "A wonderful boy, and a wonderful wedding, and a wonderful night! And now, we going to explode fireworks. We going to make the whole night explode for my two children! Is everybody ready?"

And the wedding guests cheered as Marty Sokolin lowered the muzzle of the rifle to the window sill and leveled his sights on Tommy Giordano's head.

Chapter 14

IF POLICE WORK is half doggedness and half patience, it is also half luck and half blind faith. Four halves, obviously, equal two wholes. Two holes were what Meyer

Meyer and Bob O'Brien needed in their heads the way
they needed the legwork they were doing in tracking down
Marty Sokolin.

Meyer Meyer would have been extremely content to
have lingered in the delicatessen sniffing of the savory
smells there, rather than to leave the place in search of
a potential killer. The smells of a delicatessen, especially
a kosher delly, had always been mysterious, intriguing
scents to Meyer. When he was a boy, he had no idea that
people actually went into delicatessens to make purchases.
His mother would take him for a stroll away from their
Gentile neighborhood, into the nearest ghetto, and there
she would seek out a delicatessen. Standing in the door
to the shop, she would allow little Meyer to sniff to his
heart's content. Until the time he was fifteen and bought
his first *nickel a shtickel,* Meyer held the unshakable conviction that delicatessens were for smelling only. He still
felt rather uneasy when making a purchase in one, somewhat like a heathen defiling a temple.

He did not make a purchase in the delicatessen on
Dover Plains Avenue. He made inquiries concerning the
man with the trombone case, was promptly rebuffed, and
then went into the street in further search of what was
beginning to look like a rather elusive needle. The search
was conducted in a very scientific manner based on established investigatory technique. The search was conducted
by stopping passers-by and asking them if they had seen a
man carrying a trombone case.

Now such painstaking investigatory technique is surely
recommended by Scotland Yard and the Nassau County
Police and the Sureté and the Gestapo. It is calculated to
separate, through a process of carefully phrased questions (such as, "Did you see a man with a trombone case
walk by here?) those citizens who had and those who had
not witnessed the passage of the sought suspect. It was
important, of course, to snap off the questions with the
properly authoritative and universally accepted police

tone. Police tone is a part of police procedure. The sentence, "Did you see a man with a trombone case walk by here?" when delivered by a layman untrained in police tone could result in a plethora of confused answers. When delivered by a man who had attended the Police Academy, a man well versed in the ways of investigatory technique, a man skilled at the art of interrogation, the question assumed significance. Faced with its scientific inevitability, the person questioned was skillfully led to the point where only one of two answers was possible: yes or no. I did, or I did not see a man with a trombone case walk by here.

Meyer Meyer and Bob O'Brien, skilled inquisitors that they were, received a total of twelve "no's" before they received a "yes."

The "yes" led them up a street parallel to Charles Avenue. On the front stoop of a two-story frame dwelling, they got their second "yes" and began to feel that their luck she was running good. The second "yes" came from an old man with an ear trumpet.

"Did you see a man with a trombone case walk by here?" Meyer asked scientifically.

"What?" the old man yelled. "I'm a little deaf."

"A man with a trombone case?"

"Got one inside if you want to use it," the old man said.

"A trombone?"

"Yep. On the hall table. Just dial any number you want. This ain't an out-of-town call, is it?"

"No, no, a trombone," Meyer said patiently. "A musical instrument."

"Oh, a trombone. Yes, yes. What about it?"

"Did you see a man carrying one?"

"Fellow that walked by earlier this afternoon, you mean?"

"You saw him?"

"Yep. Walked right up the street."

"Thanks," Meyer said gratefully. "That's swell. Thanks a lot."

"You can go to hell yourself, young man," the man with the ear trumpet said. "I was only trying to be helpful."

Night was falling. The sky was a multicolored bowl, light blue to the west where the sun had dropped below the horizon, a deeper blue above that, the blue of a sailor's eyes, and above that a blue that was almost black, drenched with stars, the velvet, diamond-sprinkled sheath of a sexy blonde in an all-night bistro.

"We're close to the Carella house, aren't we?" O'Brien asked.

"Charles Avenue is the next block," Meyer said.

"Think we're getting close?"

"Maybe. I'm getting tired, that's for sure."

"There's another customer," O'Brien said. "Shall we ask him?"

"We've asked everybody else so far. Why begin discriminating at this point?"

The new customer was an eight-year-old boy. He sat on the curb with a penknife. He kept throwing the penknife into the air and watching it land, handle first, into the patch of earth in front of him. It did not seem to occur to him that a slight shift of the knife would have allowed it to enter the earth blade first. The boy seemed quite content to simply throw it into the air and have it land with a sickening thud. Over and over again, he repeated the impotent act. Meyer and O'Brien watched him for a while.

"Hello, little fellow," Meyer said at last.

The boy looked up. His face was dirt-smeared in the fading light.

"Drop dead," he said.

Meyer laughed feebly. "Now, now, little fellow," he said, "we only want to ask you a question."

"Yeah? What's that?"

Meyer phrased the question carefully. "Did you see a man with a trombone case walk by here?"

The boy pierced him with stiletto eyes. "Drop dead," he said. "Can't you see I'm busy?"

"Trying to get the knife to stick into the ground?" O'Brien asked pleasantly.

"Don't be a jerk," the boy said. "Anybody can do that. I got a caterpillar here in this hole."

"A caterpillar?" O'Brien said.

"Sure. I'm trying to see how many times I can clobber him before he dies. I clobbered him thirty-four times already, and he's still moving."

"Have you tried stepping on him?" Meyer said.

"Where's the fun in that?" the boy asked.

"About this man with the trombone case, did you happen to see him go by?"

"Sure," the boy said. He picked up the knife and dropped the stubby handle onto the caterpillar's back. "Thirty-five," he said.

"Where did he go?"

"Probably up to the wedding on the next block."

"What makes you say that?"

"Thirty-six," the boy said as he dropped the knife again. "I think he's getting weak."

"What makes you think the man went to the wedding?" Meyer said.

"Because he probably cut through the back yard. Either that, or he went into the house."

"What house?"

"He was heading that way, anyway. He stopped on the sidewalk and turned in right there," the boy said. "Thirty-seven. So he either cut across the back yard to play at the wedding, or else he went inside. What else could he of done? Thirty-eight. I can count all the way to a hundred."

"Which house?" Meyer said.

"Birnbaum's," the boy answered. "The third house on

your right." He looked down into the hole. "I think I got the bastard," he said. "Wow, look at all that gook come out of him."

Meyer and O'Brien did not pause to look at the gook. Hastily, they started up the street toward the Birnbaum house. In the distance, they could hear the beginning of a faint rumbling sound—like faraway thunder.

"Can you see him?"

Him, him, him, him, him . . .

"Yes. I've got him in the sights."

Sights, sights, sights, sights, sights . . .

Don't miss this time, I won't, take careful aim, I will, they're starting the fireworks now, the little ones, I don't like the sound of fireworks, reminds me of guns going off, I hate guns going off, Marty, shut up, concentrate on what you're doing, I am, look they're setting off the pinwheels, can you still see him, yes, don't fire until the big ones go off, we need the cover of the explosions, don't fire yet, Marty, I won't, I won't.

Won't, won't, words, words, people talking, jumble of words, thunder in the distance, gunshots, fire, don't, won't . . .

Cotton Hawes climbed the echoing tunnel of unconsciousness, voices and sounds blurred meaninglessly, reverberating inside his head as blackness gave way to brightness, pinwheeling brightness outside, fireworks, yes, fireworks going off outside in the . . .

He blinked his eyes.

He tried to move.

He was trussed like Aunt Sadie's roast; his hands tied to his feet behind him, he sprawled on the floor like the base of a big rocking horse. By turning his head, he could see the window. Beyond the window, the bright dizzy gleam of the fireworks split the night air. Silhouetted in the window was Neanderthal, squatting over the rifle, and standing above him, one hand on his shoulder, leaning over slightly, the red silk stretched taut over her magnificent buttocks, was the girl who'd clonked him with the shoe.

"Take careful aim, Marty," she whispered.

"I am, I am, I've got him. Don't worry."

"Wait for the big ones. The noisy ones."

"Yes. Yes."

"You can do it, Marty."

"I know."

"You're a man, Marty. You're my man."

"I know. Shhh. Shhh. Don't make me nervous."

"When it's over, Marty. You and me. Take careful aim."

"Yes, yes."

He's going to shoot Tommy, Hawes thought helplessly. *Oh my God, he's going to shoot Tommy, and I can't do a goddamn thing to stop him.*

"What . . . what happened?" Ben Darcy asked.

He pulled away from the wet cloth Carella held in his hand. He blinked and sat upright, and then suddenly clutched his head.

"Oh, my head. Oh Jesus, it's killing me. What happened?"

"Suppose you tell me," Carella said. "Here, keep this wet cloth on the swelling."

"Yeah. Thanks." He blinked again, puzzled. "What's . . . what's all that noise?"

"They're beginning the fireworks."

"Have . . . have Tommy and Angela left yet?"

"I don't think so."

"Oh."

"Tell me what happened," Carella said.

"I'm not too sure. I was walking out back here when . . ."

"Why?"

"Why what?"

"What were you doing back here in the bushes?"

"I wasn't feeling so hot. All the confusion in there, and the row I had with Tommy. So I came here where it was a little more quiet."

"Then what?"

"Somebody hit me."

"Who?"

"I don't know."

"You yelled first," Carella said. "You yelled for help. Why'd you do that?"

"Because somebody grabbed me around the neck. That was when I yelled. My God, what did he hit me with? It feels as if my head is broken."

"It was a man, Ben?"

"Yes. Yes, it felt like a man's arm around my neck."

"And you yelled for help?"

"Yes."

"Did the man say anything?"

"Yes."

"What did he say?"

"He said, 'You lousy son of a bitch, I'm going to kill every one of you.'"

"What kind of a voice did he have?"

"Deep. Husky. He sounded like a big man."

"How big?"

"Very big. His arm was strong."

"How tall are you, Ben?"

"An even six feet."

"Would you say he was very much bigger than you? From what you could tell?"

"No, not that big. I mean, maybe six-two, six-four, something like that."

"And he said, 'You lousy son of a bitch, I'm going to kill every one of you.' Is that right?"

"That's right."

"And then he hit you?"

"Yes."

"On the head?"

"Yes."

"Is that the only place he hit you?"

"Yes."

"He didn't knock you to the ground and kick you or anything?"

"No."

"He simply put his arm around your neck, pulled you backwards, and then hit you on the top of the head, is that right?"

"Yes."

"What was he wearing?"

"A tuxedo, I think. I only saw his arm, but I think it was the sleeve of a tuxedo."

"You saw this?"

"Yes."

"It wasn't too dark to see?"

"No. No."

"What color was the tuxedo?"

"Black."

"Not blue?"

"No. Black."

"You could tell that? In the darkness here? Under the shade of the tree here?"

"Yes. It was black. I think it was black."

"And the man spoke and then hit you? Or did you yell for help first? Which?"

"First he spoke, then I . . . no, wait. I yelled for help first, and then he cursed at me, and then he hit me.

"Only once, right?"

"Yes. He hit me on the head. That's the last thing I remember."

"And you fell down unconscious, right?"

"Yes."

"One last question, Ben?"

"Yes?"

"Why are you lying to me?"

The pinwheels had sputtered out, and the Roman candles had filled the night with red. And now, standing behind the platform, the caterers from Weddings–Fetes, Incorporated, stood at the ready, anxious to light the fuses for the grand finale. Tommy Giordano stood alongside his father-in-law and his bride, bathed in the light from the bandstand, waiting for the medley of explosion and light which would come in the next few moments. He did not know that the crosshairs of a telescopic sight were fixed at a point just above his left eye. He smiled pleasantly as the caterers rushed around behind the platform, squeezed Angela's hand when he saw the first fuse being touched.

The fuse burned shorter, shorter, and then touched the powder. The first of the rockets sailed skyward, exploding in a shower of blue and green stars, followed by the second rocket almost instantly afterward, silver fishes darting against the velvet night. Explosions rocked the peaceful suburb of Riverhead, shockingly loud explosions which threatened to rip the night to shreds.

In the attic room, Oona Blake dug her fingers into Sokolin's shoulder.

"Now," she said. "Now, Marty."

Chapter 15

THE MEN WORKED together as a highly efficient team, and perhaps everything would have gone smoothly, bloodlessly, had not Bob O'Brien been a part of the team. It was certain that once the men returned to the squadroom, legend and superstition would prevail to single out O'Brien as the culprit.

They had drawn their service revolvers on the front porch of the Birnbaum house. O'Brien stood to one side of the door, and Meyer turned the knob and eased the door open. The living room on the ground floor of the house was dark and silent. Cautiously, both men entered the room.

"If he's here and plans to use a rifle," Meyer whispered, "he must be upstairs."

They waited until their eyes grew accustomed to the darkness. They found the staircase then and began climbing it, hesitating when their weight caused the treads to creak. On the second floor, they checked the two bedrooms and found them empty.

"An attic?" O'Brien whispered, and they continued climbing.

They were in the hallway outside the attic room when the fireworks started in the Carella back yard. At first, they thought it was gunfire, and then they recognized it for what it was, and both instantly formed the conclusion that their sniper—if he were indeed in the house—had undoubtedly been waiting for the fireworks before opening up with his rifle. They did not speak to each other. There was no need to speak. The operation they were about to perform had been acted out by them hundreds of times before, either together, or as part of other teams. The fireworks in the yard across the way simply added urgency to the operation but they moved swiftly and without panic, Meyer flattening himself against the wall to the right of the door, O'Brien bracing himself against the corridor wall opposite the door. O'Brien glanced at Meyer, and Meyer nodded soundlessly.

From inside the room, they heard a woman's voice say, "Now. Now, Marty."

O'Brien shoved himself off the wall, his left leg coming up, the left foot colliding with the door in a powerful, flat-footed kick that splintered the lock and shot the door inward. Like a fullback following a line plunge, O'Brien followed the door into the room, Meyer crossing in behind him like a quarterback ready to take a lateral pass.

O'Brien was not anxious to fire.

His gun was in his hand as he entered the room, following the jet-catapult of the door, his eyes sweeping first to the window where the man crouched over the rifle, then to the floor where Cotton Hawes lay tied in a neat bundle, and then back to the window again as the blonde in the red silk dress whirled to face him.

"Drop the piece!" he shouted, and the man at the window swung around with the rifle in his hands, the rockets exploding behind him in the back yard illuminating his eyes, pinpointing his eyes wth fiery light; and O'Brien's eyes locked with his, and in that moment he weighed the necessity for firing.

"Drop it!" he shouted, his eyes locked with the other man's, and he studied those eyes for the space of three seconds which seemed like three thousands years, studied the fright in them, and then the sudden awakening to the situation, and the rapid calculation. And then the eyes began to narrow and O'Brien had seen the instantaneous narrowing of the eyes of a man with a gun before, and he knew the eyes were telegraphing the action of the trigger finger, and he knew that if he did not fire instantly, he would drop to the floor bleeding in the next split second.

Meyer Meyer had seen the eyes tightening, too, and he shouted, "Watch it, Bob!" and O'Brien fired.

He fired only once, from the hip, fired with a calmness that gave the lie to the lurching beat of his heart and the trembling of his legs. His slug took Sokolin in the shoulder at close range, spinning him around and slamming him up against the wall, the rifle dropping from his hands.

And all O'Brien could think was *Don't let him die, Dear God don't let him die!*

The blonde hesitated for a fraction of an instant. With Sokolin slowly crumpling from the wall to the floor, with Meyer rushing into the room, with the world outside disintegrating in a shower of sparks and a cacophonous welter of explosions, she made her decision and acted upon it, dropping instantly to her knees, pulling the skirt back in a completely feminine gesture as she stooped with masculine purposefulness to pick up the rifle.

Meyer kicked her twice. He kicked her once to knock the rifle upward before her finger found the trigger, and then he kicked out at her legs, knocking her backward to the floor in a jumble of white flesh and sliding red silk. She came off the floor like a banshee out of hell, lips skinned back, fingers curled to rake. She wasn't looking for conversation, and Meyer didn't give her any. He swung his .38 up so that the barrel was nested in his curled fingers, the butt protruding below. Then he brought the gun around in a side-swinging arc which clipped the girl on the side of the jaw. She threw her arms and her head back, and she let out a slight whimper, and then she came down slowly, slowly, like the *Queen Mary* sinking in the River Harb, dropping to the floor in a curious mixture of titanic collapse and fragile gracefulness.

O'Brien was already crouched over Sokolin in the corner. Meyer wiped his brow.

"How is he?"

"He's hurt," O'Brien answered. "But he isn't dead."

"I knew there'd be shooting," Meyer said simply. He turned to where Cotton Hawes lay on the floor in his rocking-horse position. "Well, well," he said, "what have we here? Take a look at this, Bob."

"Get me out of these ropes," Hawes said.

"It talks, Bob," Meyer said. "Why, I do believe it's a talking dog. Now isn't that a curiosity!"

"Come on, Meyer," Hawes pleaded, and Meyer saw his

battered face for the first time, and quickly stooped to cut the binding ropes. Hawes rose. Massaging his wrists and ankles, he said, "You got here just in the nick."

"The Marines always arrive on time," Meyer said.

"And the U.S. Cavalry," O'Brien answered. He glanced at the blonde. "She's got crazy legs," he said.

The men studied her appreciatively for a moment.

"So," Meyer said at last, "I guess this is it. We'll need the meat wagon for that joker, won't we?"

"Yeah," O'Brien said listlessly.

"You want to make the call, Bob?"

"Yeah, okay."

He left the room. Meyer walked to the blonde and clamped his handcuffs onto her wrists. With a married man's dispassionate aloofness, he studied her exposed legs for the last time, and then pulled down her skirt. "There," he said. "Decency and morality prevail once more. She had a wild look in her eye, that one. I wouldn't have wanted to mess with her."

"I *did*," Hawes said.

"Mmm." Meyer looked at his face. "I think maybe we got another passenger for the meat wagon. You don't look exactly beautiful, dear lad."

"I don't feel exactly beautiful," Hawes said.

Meyer holstered his revolver. "Nothing like a little excitement on a Sunday, is there?"

"What the hell are *you* kicking about?" Hawes asked. "This is *my* day off."

"Lying?" Ben Darcy said. "What do you mean? Why would I . . . ?"

"Come on, Ben. Over to the house," Carella said.

"What for? What did I . . . ?" A gun magically appeared in Carella's fist. Darcy studied it for a moment and then said, "Jesus, you're serious, aren't you?"

"Aren't *you*?" Carella asked, and together they walked out of the bushes. The fireworks were exploding behind them, the sighs of the crowd following each new display of pyrotechnic wizardry. Kling met the pair at the house.

"I've been looking for you, Steve," he said. "It's past eight, and I'm supposed to pick up Claire at nine. So I'd better be taking off."

"Hang around a few more minutes, would you, Bert?"

"What for?"

"Hang around, can you?"

"Okay, but you don't know Claire when I'm late."

"Inside," Carella said to Darcy. They entered the house. "Upstairs." They went upstairs to the room that had been Carella's when he was a boy. School pennants still decorated the walls. Airplane models hung from the ceiling. A Samurai sword he'd sent home from the Pacific was hung to the right of the windows, near the desk. In the room where he'd been a boy, Carella felt no nostalgic wistfulness. He had led Darcy into the privacy of the house because he was about to conduct a police interrogation, and he wanted the psychological advantage of the cloistered silence, the four walls, all the appearance of a trap. At the 87th, he'd have used the small Interrogation Room set close to the Clerical Office, and for the same reasons. There were some cops who used the Interrogation Room as a sparring ring, but Carella had never laid a hand on a prisoner in all the years he'd been a cop, and he did not intend to start now. But he recognized his weapons, and he knew that Darcy was lying, and he wanted to know now *why* he was lying. He had drawn his gun with the same psychological warfare in mind. He knew he did not need his gun with Darcy. But the gun added official police weight. And, in following through on his line of intent, he had asked Kling to accompany him upstairs because the police weight was doubled with a second cop along; the feeling of inevitable exposure mounted, the lie would root around in the suspect's mind searching for a rock beneath which to hide, relentlessly exposed to the overwhelming odds against it.

"Sit down," he said to Darcy.

Darcy sat.

"Why do you want Tommy dead?" Carella asked bluntly.

"What?"

"You heard me." He stood to the right of Darcy's chair. Kling, knowing what was happening, immediately assumed a position to the left of the chair.

"Tommy *dead?*" Darcy said. "Are you kidding me? Why would I . . . ?"

"That's what I asked you."

"But I . . ."

"You said a man slightly taller than you came up behind you in the bushes and circled your neck with his arm, is that right?"

"Yes. Yes, that's the truth."

"And then he hit you on the head, right? Once? Right?"

"Yes. That's what happened. How does that . . . ?"

"I'm six feet tall," Carella said, "give or take a quarter of an inch. Bert here is about six-two. That's about the difference in height between you and your alleged attacker, isn't it? Isn't that what you said?"

"Yes, that's what I . . ."

"Would you mind grabbing me from behind, Bert? Put your arm far enough around me so that I can see what kind of clothes you're wearing. You *did* tell me your attacker was wearing a tuxedo, didn't you?"

"Well, I . . ."

"Didn't you?"

"Yes," Darcy said.

"Okay, Bert."

Kling wrapped his arm around Carella's neck. Carella stood facing Darcy, the gun in his right hand.

"We're pretty close, aren't we, Darcy? I'm practically

smack up against him. In fact, it would be impossible for Bert to take a whack at my head unless he shoved me on the head this way. Am I right?"

"Yes, that's right," Darcy said quickly. "The attacker *did* shove me away from him. I remember that now. I yelled and then just before he hit me, he shoved me a few feet away from him. So that he could swing. That's right. That's just the way it happened."

"Well, that's different," Carella said, smiling. "Why didn't you say so in the first place? So he shoved you away from him, right?"

"Yes."

"Would you mind demonstrating that, Bert?"

Kling shoved out gently at Carella, and Carella stepped forward a few paces. "About like that?" he asked Darcy.

"Well, with considerably more force. But that's about where I wound up, yes. A few feet ahead of him."

"Well, you should have told me that to begin with," Carella said, still smiling. "He hit you from a few feet behind you, right?"

"Yes."

"That makes a big difference," Carella said, smiling pleasantly. "And he didn't kick you or anything, am I right?"

"That's right," Darcy said, nodding. "He pushed me away from him and then he hit me. That was all."

"Then suppose you tell me, Ben, why the hell that cut is in the exact center of your skull, on the top of your head? Suppose you tell me that, Ben?"

"What? I don't—"

"If you were hit from behind, you'd most likely have been hit either on the side or the back of your head. Unless the man who hit you was an absolute giant, the cut would not be in the *center* of your skull. The size man you described would never have been able to get force enough into a blow that presupposes his extending the weapon above your head and then bringing it down vertically."

"He . . . he was bigger than I thought."

"How big?"

"Six-six, maybe. Maybe bigger."

"That isn't big enough! The natural swing of his arm would have brought that gun down on a slant at the back of your head. Or, if he took a side swing, at either the right or the left of your head, behind the ears. How about it, Darcy? The wound was self-inflicted, wasn't it? You ducked your head and ran into that big maple, didn't you?"

"No, no, why would I want to—?"

"To throw suspicion away from yourself. Because you sawed through that tie rod end!" Kling said.

"You were out for a walk this morning, weren't you? That's what you told me when I first saw you," Carella said.

"Yes, but—"

"Did you run yourself into that tree? Did you saw through that tie rod end on your little stroll?"

"No, no, I . . ."

"Did you send Tommy that black widow spider?"

"No, no, I swear I didn't do any of—"

"A note came with the spider," Carella shouted. "We'll compare your handwriting—"

"My handwriting? . . . But I didn't . . ."

"Is that blonde in this with you?" Kling shouted.

"What blonde?"

"The one whose gun killed Birnbaum!"

"Birnbaum!"

"Or did you kill Birnbaum?"

"I didn't kill anybody. I only—"

"Only what?"

"I only wanted to—"

"To what?"

"I . . . I . . ."

"Take him away, Bert," Carella snapped. "Book him for the murder of the old man. Premeditated homicide. It's an open-and-shut Murder One."

"Murder?" Darcy shouted, "I didn't touch the old man! I only wanted—"

"*What* did you want? Goddamnit, Darcy, spit it out!"

"I . . . I . . . I only wanted to scare Tommy at first. With . . . with the spider. I . . . I thought maybe I'd scare him enough so that he'd . . . he'd back out of the wedding. But . . . he . . . he didn't, he wouldn't . . . he wouldn't scare."

"So you went to work on the car, right?"

"Yes, but not to *kill* him! I didn't want to *kill* him!"

"What the hell did you think would happen when that rod snapped?"

"An accident, I thought, to stop the wedding, but that . . . that didn't work, either. And then I—"

"Where does the blonde come in?"

"I don't know any blonde. I don't know what you're talking about."

"The blonde who shot Birnbaum! Come clean, Darcy!"

"I'm telling you everything. I was only trying to scare Tommy. The wine was to make him sick, yes, but then I took Angela for a ride in my car, and I tried to talk sense to her. If she'd agreed to what I . . ."

"What wine? What do you mean, wine?"

"The wine. For him and her. And if Angela had told me she'd go along with me, I'd have taken the bottles back. But anyway, it's only to make him sick, so he'll . . . he'll look like a boob on his honeymoon. So she'll be . . . disgusted with him. And then maybe she'll come to me, after all. I love her, Stevel I love Angela!"

"You gave them wine?"

"Two bottles. One for him, and one for her. To take on the honeymoon. Two small little bottles, I left them on the bridal table. With cards."

"Where'd you get the wine?"

"My father makes it. He makes a barrel each year."

"And bottles it?"

"Yes."

"You put something in that wine? To make them sick?"

"Only Tommy's bottle. Only the one marked 'For the Groom.' I wouldn't want Angela to get sick. That's why I put two separate bottles on the table. One for the bride and one for the groom. Only *his* bottle has the stuff in it."

"What stuff?"

"You don't have to worry. It'll only make him sick. I only used a little of it."

"A little of *what*, goddammit!"

"The stuff we use in the garden. To kill weeds. But I only put it in Tommy's bottle. I wouldn't want Angela to—"

"Weed killer? Weed killer?" Carella shouted. "With an arsenic base?"

"I don't know what it had in it. I only used a little. Just to make him get sick."

"Didn't it say POISON on the can?"

"Yes, but I only used a little. Just to—"

"How much did you use?"

"It was just a small bottle of wine. I put in about half a cupful."

"Half a—and you mix that stuff twenty to one with water to kill weeds! And you put half a cup of it into Tommy's wine! That'd kill an army!"

"Kill an—but—but—but I only wanted to make him sick. And only him. Not Angela. Only him."

"They're married now, you goddamn idiot! They'll drink from *one* bottle or *both* bottles or . . . you god-damn fool! What makes you think they're going to follow your instructions for a honeymoon toast! Oh, you god-damn idiot! Cuff him to the radiator, Bert! I've got to stop the kids!"

Chapter 16

DANCING HAD COMMENCED under a starlit sky.

The Sal Martino Orchestra, having imbibed of good, clean, commercially bottled wines and champagnes and whiskies all afternoon and evening, having been treated to the sweet, exhilarating taste of Antonio Carella's expensive elixir, played with a magnificently mellow lilt. Distant cousins embraced distant cousins with mounting fervor as the hours ran out. It would be a long time before the next wedding.

Steve Carella burst from the house and onto the dance floor, his eyes skirting his wife where she sat wriggling uncomfortably in her chair, darting over the dance floor in search of Tommy and Angela. They were nowhere in sight. He saw his mother dancing with Uncle Garibaldi from Scranton, and he rushed over to her and pulled her from the startled uncle's arms and said, "Where are the kids?"

"What?" Louisa said.

"Tommy and Angela. Where are they?"

Louisa Carella winked.

"Mama, they didn't *leave*, did they?"

Louisa Carella, who'd had a bit of the commercially bottled elixir herself, winked again.

"Mama, did they leave?"

"Yes, yes, they left. This is their wedding. What did you want them to do? Stand around and talk to the old folks?"

"Oh, Mama!" Carella said despairingly. "Did you see them go?"

"Yes, of course I saw them. I kissed Angela goodbye."

"Were they carrying anything?"

"Suitcases, naturally. They're going on a honeymoon, you know."

"*Che cosa?*" Uncle Garibaldi from Scranton asked.

"*Che cosa, Louisa?*"

"*Niente. Sia zitto, Garibaldi,*" she answered him, and then turned to her son. "What's the matter?"

"Somebody put two small bottles of homemade wine on the table this afternoon. Did you happen to see them?"

"Yes. His and Hers. Very cute."

"Did they have that wine with them when they left?"

"Yes. Yes, I think so. Yes, I saw Tommy put the bottles in one of the suitcases."

"Oh, Jesus!" Carella said.

"Steve! I don't like you to swear."

"Where'd they go, Mama?"

"Go? How should I know? This is their honeymoon. Did you tell me where *you* went on your honeymoon?"

"Oh, Jesus," Carella said again. "What did she tell me, what did she say? She *talked* about the hotel! Damnit, what did she say? Did she mention the name?"

"What's the matter with you?" Louisa asked her son. "You act like a crazy man!"

"Bert!" Carella shouted, and Kling ran to where he was standing. "Bert, did you hear anybody mention the name of the hotel the kids were going to?"

"No? Why? Have they left with the wine?"

"Yes."

"Oh, Jesus," Kling said.

"What do we do?"

"I don't know."

"A big hotel, she said. I'm sure she said that. Hold it, hold it. One of the biggest hotels in the world, she said. Right in this city. She said that." He clutched Kling's

"Which is one of the biggest hotels in the world, Bert?"

"I don't know," Kling said helplessly.

"Do you think someone might have seen them drive away?" He turned to his mother. "Mama, did they take a car?"

"No, a taxi, Steve. What *is* the matter? Why are you . . . ?"

"*Che cosa?*" Uncle Garibaldi from Scranton asked again.

"*Sia zitto!*" Louisa said more firmly.

"Did you hear Tommy tell the taxi driver where they were going?"

"No. My God, they only left a few minutes ago. If I knew it was important, I'd have asked them to . . ."

But Carella had left his mother and was running toward the front of the house and the sidewalk. He stopped at the gate and looked in both directions. Kling pulled up to a puffing halt beside him.

"See anything?"

"No."

"There's somebody."

Carella looked to where Jody Lewis, the photographer, was packing his equipment into the trunk of his car.

"Lewis," he said. "Maybe he saw them. Come on."

They walked to the car. Lewis slammed the trunk shut and then came around the side of the car quickly. "Nice wedding," he said, and he got into the car and started the engine.

"Just a second," Carella said. "Did you see my sister and her husband leave here?"

"The happy couple?" Lewis said. "Yes, indeed. Excuse me, but I'm in a hurry." He released the hand brake.

"Did you happen to overhear the address they gave the cab driver?"

"No, I did not," Lewis said. "I am not in the habit of eavesdropping. Now, if you'll excuse me, I want to finish my work and get to bed. Good night. It was a wonderful wedding."

"Finish your . . . ?" Carella started, and he turned to Kling, and the same excited look crossed both their faces in the same instant. "You going to take another picture of them?"

"Yes, I'm . . ."

"At the hotel? Putting their shoes out?"

"Yes," Lewis said, "so you can see I'm in a hurry. If you'll . . ."

"You've got company, mister," Carella said, and he threw open the car door. Kling piled into the sedan. Carella was following him when he heard his mother's voice on the path behind him.

"Steve! Steve!"

He hesitated, one foot inside the car, the other on the pavement.

"What is it, Mama?"

"Teddy! It's Teddy! It's her time!"

"What?"

"Her time! The baby, Steve!"

"But the baby isn't due until next we—"

"It's her time!" Louisa Carella said firmly. "Get her to the hospital!"

Carella slammed the car door shut. He thrust his head through the open window and shouted, "Stop the kids, Bert! My wife's gonna have a baby!" and he ran like hell up the path to the house.

"What hotel is it?" Kling asked.

"The Neptune."

"Can't you drive any faster?"

"I'm driving as fast as I can. I don't want to get a ticket."

"I'm a detective," Kling said. "You can drive as fast as you want. Now step on it!"

"Yes, *sir*," Lewis answered, and he rammed his foot down on the accelerator.

"Can't you drive any faster?" Carella said to the cab driver.

"I'm driving as fast as I can," the cabbie answered.

"Dammit! My wife's about to have a baby!"

"Well, mister, I'm . . ."

"I'm a cop," Carella said. "Get this heap moving."

"What are you worried about?" the cabbie said, pressing his foot to the accelerator. "Between a cop and a cabbie, we sure as hell should be able to deliver a baby."

Chapter 17

A CONVENTION OF ELKS or Moose or Mice or Masons or something was cavorting in the lobby of the Neptune Hotel when Kling arrived with Jody Lewis. One of the Elks or Moose or Mice or whatever touched Kling with an electrically charged cane, and he leaped two feet in the air, and then rushed again toward the reception desk, thinking he would arrest that man as a public menace as soon as he finished this business with Tommy and Angela. God, it was past eight-thirty, Claire would have a fit when he finally got around to picking her up. Assuming the kids hadn't tasted that wine yet—why was he calling them kids? Tommy was about his age—but assuming they hadn't tasted the wine, assuming a stomach pump and a rush to the hospital wouldn't be necessary, holy Moses what had happened to what had started out as a quiet Sunday?

"Mr. and Mrs. Giordano," he said to the desk clerk.

"Yes, sir, they checked in a little while ago," the clerk answered.

"What room are they in?"

"I'm sorry, sir, they left instructions not to be disturbed. They're honeymooners, you see, and . . ."

"I'm from the police department," Kling said, snapping open his wallet to his shield. "What room? Quick!"

"Is something . . . ?"

"What room, dammit?"

"428. Is something . . . ?"

Kling rushed to the elevator. Behind him, camera in hand, Jody Lewis dashed across the lobby.

"Four," Kling said to the elevator boy. "Hurry!"

"What's the rush?" the boy answered. Idling against the control panel, he gave Kling a bored sneer. Kling didn't feel like arguing. Nor did he feel like earning the distinction of being the first Neptune guest to be treated with rudeness in the past ten years. He simply clutched one hand in the elevator boy's tunic, yanked him away from the control panel, slammed him against the rear wall of the elevator just as Jody Lewis entered the car, and then pressed the button to close the doors and pressed another button marked with the numeral 4.

"Hey," the elevator boy said, "you're not allowed to——"

"Just shut the hell up," Kling said, "or I'll throw you down the shaft."

The boy modulated into an injured silence. Sulking against the rear wall of the elevator, he silently cursed Kling as the car sped up the shaft. The doors slid open and Kling rushed into the hall with Lewis. Behind him, in a parting shot of defiance, the elevator boy yelled, "You louse!" and then hastily closed the doors.

"What room?" Lewis asked.

"428."

"This way."

"No, this way."

"It says 420 to 428 here."

"The arrow's pointing this way."

They rushed down the hall together.

"Here it is!" Lewis said.

Kling rapped on the door. "Open up!" he shouted.

"Who's there?" Tommy's voice shouted back.

"Police! Bert Kling! Open up! Hurry!"

"What? What?" Tommy said, his voice puzzled behind the wood of the door. A lock was thrown back. A key turned. The door opened. Tommy stood there with a wine glass in one hand. He was wearing a blue silk robe, and he seemed terribly embarrassed. Behind him, sitting in a love seat, Angela Giordano tilted a wine glass to her lips as she watched the door with a perplexed frown on her forehead.

Kling's eyes opened wide. "Stop!" he shouted.

"Wh—?"

"Don't drink that wine!"

He darted into the room past a startled Tommy Giordano, and then slapped the wine glass out of Angela's hands.

"Hey, what the hell . . ." Tommy started and Kling said, "Did you drink any?"

"The wine?"

"Yes, yes, the wine!"

"No. We just opened one of the bottles. What . . ?"

"Which one?"

"I don't know. They're both on the table there. What is this? Did the fellows put you up to this?"

Kling ran to the table and lifted the open bottle of wine. The card still hung from its neck. *For the Bride.* Suddenly, he felt like a horse's ass. He picked up the second bottle, the one marked *For the Groom* and, greatly embarrassed, he started for the door.

"Excuse me," he said. "Sorry to bust in on you. Wine was no good. Sorry. Excuse me, excuse me," he said, backing toward the door.

Behind him, Jody Lewis said, "One last picture, please. Just put your shoes in the hall for me, would you? One last picture?"

"Oh, go to hell," Tommy said, and he slammed the door on his visitors.

"Boy," Lewis said, "what a temper." He paused. "Is that wine you've got there?"

"Yes," Kling said, still embarrassed.

"Why don't we open it and have a drink?" Lewis said.

"I'm exhausted."

Steve Carella paced the floor of the hospital waiting room. Meyer, Hawes, and O'Brien who'd followed the meat wagon and Sokolin to the hospital after depositing Oona Blake with the local precinct, paced the floor behind him.

"What's taking so long?" Carella asked. "My God, does it always take this long?"

"Relax," Meyer said. "I've been through this three times already. It gets longer each time."

"She's been up there for close to an hour," Carella moaned.

"She'll be all right, don't worry. What are you going to name the baby?"

"Mark if it's a boy, and April if it's a girl, Meyer, it shouldn't be taking this long, should it?"

"Relax."

"Relax, relax," He paused. "I wonder if Kling got to the kids in time."

"Relax," Meyer said.

"Can you imagine a nut like that? Putting arsenic— half a cup of it—into a small bottle of wine and thinking it would only make Tommy *sick*! A dental student! Is that what they teach dentists about chemistry?" He shook his head. "Attempted murder, I make it. We throw the book at the bastard."

"Relax," Meyer said. "We'll throw the book at all of them."

"How's Sokolin making out?"

"He'll live," Meyer said. "Did you see Cotton's face?"

"I hear a girl beat you up, Cotton," Carella said.

"Yeah," Hawes said shamefacedly.

"Here comes a nurse," O'Brien said.

Carella whirled. With starched precision, the nurse marched down the corridor. He walked rapidly to greet her, his heels clicking on the marble floor.

"Is she all right?" the detectives heard him ask, and the nurse nodded and then took Carella's arm and brought him to the side of the corridor where they entered into a whispered consultation. Carella kept nodding. The detectives watched him. Then, in a louder voice, Carella asked, "Can I go see her now?"

"Yes," the nurse answered. "The doctor's still with her. Everything's fine."

Carella started down the hallway, not looking back at his colleagues.

"Hey!" Meyer shouted.

Carella turned.

"What is it?" Meyer said. "Mark or April?"

And Carella, a somewhat mystified grin on his face, shouted, "Both!" and then broke into a trot for the elevators.

Fabulous Fiction From SIGNET

☐ **BRANDY KANE by Constance Gluyas.** (120019—$3.50)*
(0451)

☐ **BRIDGE TO YESTERDAY by Constance Gluyas.**
(110137—$3.50)*

☐ **FLAME OF THE SOUTH by Constance Gluyas.**
(099141—$2.95)

☐ **LORD SIN by Constance Gluyas.** (095219—$2.75)

☐ **THE PASSIONATE SAVAGE by Constance Gluyas.**
(092281—$2.95)

☐ **ROUGE'S MISTRESS by Constance Gluyas.** (110094—$2.95)

☐ **SAVAGE EDEN by Constance Gluyas.** (092856—$2.95)

☐ **WOMAN OF FURY by Constance Gluyas.** (080750—$2.25)

☐ **THE HOUSE OF KINGSLEY MERRICK by Deborah Hill.**
(089189—$2.50)

☐ **THIS IS THE HOUSE by Deborah Hill.** (112725—$2.50)

☐ **KINGSLAND by Deborah Hill.** (112636—$2.95)

☐ **ECSTASY'S EMPIRE by Gimone Hall.** (092929—$2.75)

☐ **THE JASMINE VEIL by Gimone Hall.** (114515—$2.95)

☐ **TEMPTING FATE by Chelsea Quinn Yarbro.** (118650—$3.95)*

☐ **PATH OF THE ECLIPSE by Chelsea Quinn Yarbro.**
(113403—$3.50)*

☐ **THE PALACE by Chelsea Quinn Yarbro.** (089499—$2.25)*

*Prices slightly higher in Canada

Buy them at your local bookstore or use this convenient coupon for ordering.

THE NEW AMERICAN LIBRARY, INC.
P.O. Box 999, Bergenfield, New Jersey 07621

Please send me the books I have checked above. I am enclosing $_____
(please add $1.00 to cover postage and handling). Send check
or money order—no cash or C.O.D.'s. Prices and numbers are subject to change
without notice.

Name_____

Address_____

City_____ State_____ Zip Code_____

Allow 4-6 weeks for delivery.
This offer is subject to withdrawal without notice.